A Nation Without Reservation

by Alan Maas

The Nations of the Plains— *Book 1*

This is a work of fiction. Unless otherwise indicated, all the names, characters, businesses, places, events and incidents in this book are either the product of the author's imagination or used in a fictitious manner. Any resemblance to actual persons, living or dead, or actual events is purely coincidental.

ACKNOWLEDGMENTS

Published by Alan Maas

ISBN: 979-8-9890660-6-3

Printed in the United States of America

Dedication

I would like to dedicate this book to my friends and family—without them, none of this would have been possible.
Too often, we take the people closest to us for granted, when in truth, it's their presence that shapes the experiences of our lives. I have truly been blessed.
My parents took on the incredible challenge of raising five children, each of whom turned out exceptional in their own ways. I know not everyone is fortunate enough to have strong family bonds or lifelong friendships, but I encourage you: don't give up on the people who can walk alongside you, lift you up, and share your journey.
I hope that everyone who reads my stories comes away wanting to know more. It is what keeps us going in life. So, keep breathing, smiling and moving!

About the Author

Alan Maas is a historical fiction author with a deep appreciation for the untold stories of the American frontier. Drawing inspiration from real events, forgotten legends, and his passion for the Black Hills region, Maas brings the past to life through richly imagined characters and immersive, atmospheric storytelling.

History has always fascinated me—not for the dates and numbers, which never seemed to stick, but for the stories and the way everything connects. My goal is to write stories that weave history together, making it both educational and entertaining. Every time I uncover a new piece of history; I'm amazed at how it always ties back to something we can relate to—often in ways that surprise me.

That said, research is key. There are always multiple sides to every story, and understanding the full picture requires digging deeper. As I always say, never pass up the chance to have a conversation or listen to a story—you never know where it might lead or what you'll discover!

Author's Note

This book imagines an alternate history in which the nations of the Plains unite and negotiate sovereignty after the conflicts of the 1870s. Many of the figures portrayed here—Crazy Horse, Red Cloud, Quanah Parker, and Ulysses S. Grant—were real leaders whose lives shaped the history of North America.

While the events in this book are fictionalized, the cultures, landscapes, and conflicts of the Plains are grounded in historical record. The struggles over land, sovereignty, survival, and identity were real, and their consequences continue to shape the lives of Indigenous nations today.

The idea at the heart of this story is simple but powerful: history is not inevitable. At certain moments, the decisions of leaders, the unity of nations, or the outcome of a single battle can alter the course of generations. The victory at the Battle of the Greasy Grass—known in U.S. history as the Battle of the Little Bighorn—was one such moment.

In reality, the years that followed brought increasing pressure from the United States government, the loss of land, and the confinement of Plains peoples to reservations. In this novel, however, I explore another possibility: what might have happened if the nations of the Plains had found a way to stand together long enough to secure recognition as a sovereign confederation.

This story is not meant to replace history, but to invite readers to reconsider it—to imagine how different the world might look if Indigenous nations had been allowed to determine their own future.

The Plains were never empty land.

They were home to nations.

Contents

Chapter 1 -The Year the Nation Split

1860

In the East, the country parted along lines long traced yet seldom named.

Upon the Plains the division was heard only as distant thunder. Yet thunder travels farther than sight, and men who have lived long beneath open sky do not mistake its approach.

When Abraham Lincoln was chosen president in November of 1860, the newspapers moving west along the Missouri came folded and refolded until the creases nearly split the page. Traders carried them in saddlebags darkened by grease and dust. Steamboat crews bore them upriver in damp bundles tied with cord, the ink sometimes blurred by spray. At Fort Randall soldiers read them aloud in measured tones, pausing over unfamiliar names and repeating certain phrases as though repetition might steady them.

In distant parlors men disputed Union and sovereignty.

On the Plains men counted patrols.

South Carolina withdrew first. Even along the river that much was known. Other states followed in deliberate order. Ordinances were signed. Flags were lowered and raised again beneath different colors. Militias drilled in courthouse squares and pasture fields. Each action was declared necessary. Each described as a defense of principle.

Far away, it seemed a matter of paper and speech.

Here, it altered the rhythm of hooves.

In Washington City the government turned inward upon its own fracture. The long pressure upon the frontier—surveyors measuring land by chain, soldiers riding circuit, settlers following wagon ruts deepening with each season—did not cease. Yet it slackened.

On the Plains the change was not read in headlines.

It was felt in what did not arrive.

* * *

Mato Ska did not yet comprehend what a nation was.

He understood horses and their temper. He knew the weight of a river's current and the sound ice made when it first formed along the bank. He understood also the silence adults adopted when children came too near their talk.

His name meant White Bear. He had carried it since before history required remembering him.

Their camp lay near a bend of the Missouri where the water curved broad and deliberate before turning south. Cottonwoods along the bank had thinned; leaves gathered in dry drifts against the roots. In the mornings smoke from cook fires settled low and lingered until the sun rose high enough to draw it upward.

The riders came near midday.

They were not returning from a hunt. Dust lay thick upon their leggings. One horse bore a small cut along its flank, poorly bound. The men passed their reins to waiting hands and went directly to the elders.

Mato followed at a distance, stooping now and again as if intent upon some tasks of his own.

He heard words he knew.

Wasichu.

Fort.

Soldiers.

Then another phrase, spoken plainly.

"Their own chiefs are fighting."

The words unsettled him. White men fought outward. They pressed and advanced. They did not turn their weapons upon one another.

His uncle spat lightly into the earth.

"When they quarrel among themselves," he said, "they may forget us for a time. Or they may come against us with greater force when they are finished."

Mato frowned. "How can both be so?"

No one rebuked him.

His uncle answered without raising his voice. "A wounded man does not strike with care."

That night Mato lay wrapped in a robe near the fire. Beyond the circle of light, the river moved in steady darkness. He tried to imagine white chiefs contending with white chiefs. The thought would not settle. The United States existed in his mind as weather exists—distant, powerful, inevitable.

He did not yet understand that even weather turns upon itself.

* * *

Fort Randall stood upriver upon a broad rise above the Missouri.

It was no stone fortress. Its strength lay not in walls but in arrangement. Long timber barracks faced one another across a beaten parade ground. Storehouses and officers' quarters stood in ordered lines. A flagstaff rose at the center, visible for miles in clear weather. Beyond the buildings stretched open prairie.

There was little to prevent a determined rider from crossing the grounds except the presence of armed men and the authority they claimed. More than once Lakota youths had ridden close enough to test that authority, circling beyond musket range or galloping past the outer buildings before the alarm could fully sound. The soldiers answered with discipline rather than pursuit.

From a ridge above the river Mato had often watched the post. Bugle calls carried thinly across the grass. Patrols rode out in regular number and returned at appointed hours. Supply wagons creaked in from the south, their teams blown and mud-streaked after long travel along the river road.

In the year 1860 the pattern altered.

A patrol that should have counted twelve rode forth with eight. The empty spaces in the line were easily seen against the open land. One wagon expected before frost did not arrive until snow lay in shaded hollows. A steamboat passed the landing without tying up, its paddle beating steadily as it continued downriver.

Mato and his uncle stood upon the ridge one afternoon and watched a smaller column return across the parade ground. The men dismounted without flourish and led their horses toward the stables.

"They send men away," Mato said.

His uncle inclined his head. "Yes."

"To what place?"

"To their own struggle."

The flag moved faintly above the roofs.

"If they fight there," Mato asked, "will they forget here?"

"For a season," his uncle replied.

"And afterward?"

"Afterward they will remember."

* * *

Before the first heavy snow, a trader passed through who had traveled as far as Omaha. He spoke Lakota well enough to bargain without signs and laid out his goods upon a blanket—coffee in small sacks, iron tools, bright cloth, and talk gathered along the river.

"The white men are dividing," he told the elders near the fire. "There will be war."

The word carried differently when applied to distant states than when spoken of Pawnee or Crow.

At the mention of the Crow, one of the older men shifted where he sat.

"They listen closely at the forts," he said.

Another answered, "They have long sought friends against us."

The trader shrugged. "They believe the soldiers may yet return their hunting grounds."

No one replied at once. The matter was not new, yet it bore repeating. The Crow had pressed for advantage where they could find it. The Lakota had done the same.

A third voice, low and steady, said, "Each people choose the path it believes will let it endure."

The fire cracked softly.

Mato did not grasp the full weight of the exchange, but he understood that the world beyond the river did not divide neatly between white and Lakota. Other reckonings moved beneath the surface.

Later he asked his mother, "How does a people remember itself?"

She tied off the thread in her sewing before answering.

"By knowing who they are," she said.

"And if they forget?"

She looked toward the dark river, unseen yet constant.

"Then someone must remind them."

* * *

Snow fell before all the leaves had entirely dropped.

Travel grew slow. Horses were rubbed down carefully at dusk lest frost stiffen their hides. Wood had to be gathered at greater distance as nearer stands were thinned. The river, rimmed with ice along its edges, moved black between white banks.

Mato carried what he was able. He listened more than he spoke.

One evening he sat beside the elder who kept the winter count, marking each year upon hide with a single sign. The old man's hands were deliberate.

"What shall you mark for this year?" Mato asked.

"It is not yet ended," the elder replied.

Mato thought of smaller patrols and quieter bugles, of talk carried by traders, and of Crow men riding nearer the forts than before.

"Fewer soldiers," he ventured.

The elder allowed a faint smile.

"We do not mark what departs," he said. "We mark what alters."

Mato considered this.

"What has altered?"

The elder's gaze rested upon the distant rise where the fort stood against the sky.

"Their attention," he said.

* * *

Far to the east, men affixed their names to documents and called the act necessary.

On the Plains a boy watched a post diminished in number and listened as elders weighed their words with greater care.

Two movements had begun.

One born of politics.

One sustained by patience.

The Plains did not rend as paper rends.

They endured.

And Mato Ska, without knowing that history had begun to turn in his direction, learned to listen before he spoke.

Chapter 2 -The Hunger Years

1861–1862

The first winter of the white men's war passed quietly along the Missouri.

Too quietly.

The war did not reach Mato Ska in speeches. It reached him in smaller sacks of coffee and in wagons that failed to appear. Traders who once arrived before the first hard frost came only after the ground had stiffened. Powder and lead cost more robes than before. At the post upriver the patrols rode less often, and those who did ride carried themselves differently, as though part of their attention lay far beyond the horizon.

War had begun in the East.

Names drifted west before their meaning did—Bull Run, Shiloh, Antietam. The words were spoken beside cook fires and repeated inside the long timber buildings at Fort Randall. To most upon the Plains they were not places but sounds, like distant weather rolling across country too far away to see.

Here the meaning was simpler.

Attention had shifted.

* * *

Mato was no longer a child who lingered unnoticed at the edge of council. He had grown taller; his voice no longer broke when he spoke. When riders arrived, he stepped forward without instruction—taking bridles, fetching water, rubbing down horses whose flanks were white with dried sweat. He listened carefully and spoke less.

It was early summer when a small party of Santee Dakota came west seeking kin and counsel.

They brought no gifts.

They brought hunger.

Mato perceived it before words were spoken. Their belts had been drawn tight to take in slack. Their ponies showed rib and hip beneath dull coats. Hunger clings to men even when pride remains upright.

They were received with courtesy. Meat was set before them. Water was offered first.

One of the Dakota elders spoke once they had eaten.

"The agent says the annuity is delayed," he said. "The trader refuses further credit."

A younger man, his voice held taut, added, "When we said our children were hungry, he told us they might eat grass."

The words settled heavily in the circle.

No one answered at once.

Later, when the council had broken, Mato spoke quietly to his uncle.

"The United States promised them food."

His uncle inclined his head.

"They promise often."

"And when the promise does not arrive?"

His uncle looked toward the river, broad and slow beneath the summer sun.

"Then men begin to look for other means."

***

By late summer the rumors had sharpened into fact.

Four young Dakota hunters were said to have killed settlers along the Minnesota River after a quarrel. Some claimed the dispute concerned food. Others spoke of insult. Those who had watched events for years said the cause lay deeper than any single exchange.

Whatever the spark, the prairie carried the flame.

Dakota bands struck trading posts and farmsteads. Settlers fled in crowded wagons. Local militias formed with haste and little discipline. Though the United States Army was drawn thin by its war in the East, troops were sent northward.

What had begun as disturbance became open conflict.

Mato did not witness the first blows. He saw instead the riders who carried the tidings west.

"They try our men in groups," one Dakota visitor said weeks later, his face worn and hollow. "They do not hear all the words. They do not weigh all the reasons."

"How many?" an elder asked.

The man stared into the fire as though counting faces within the coals.

"Many."

The number reached them in time.

Thirty-eight.

The executions were carried out at Mankato before a gathered crowd. A great wooden frame had been raised, and many nooses hung from it.

Mato repeated the number to himself that night.

Thirty-eight.

It was not the size of an army.

It was the weight of certainty.

***

Snow came early and lay deep.

Game grew scarce near the river bottoms and had to be sought farther out upon the plains. Wood was cut at greater distance. Travel between camps required stronger horses and greater care.

Mato again sat beside the keeper of the winter count as the old man prepared to mark the year upon hide.

The elder's hand hovered above the surface.

"What shall stand for this winter?" he asked quietly.

Mato did not answer at once.

He thought of gaunt faces, of withheld food, of ropes tightening against a winter sky.

"The day many were hanged," he said at last.

The elder regarded him.

"Why that?"

"So that we remember," Mato answered.

"Remember what?"

"That even while fighting among themselves, they found time to hang thirty-eight men."

The old man nodded once.

Upon the hide he marked a wooden frame, and beneath it small suspended figures drawn with careful strokes.

* * *

Among the Lakota there was anger, yet it did not burst its bounds.

This surprised Mato.

He had expected fury to move north like fire in dry grass. Instead, councils lengthened and voices lowered. Men counted rifles. They counted horses fit for war. They observed the number of soldiers at Fort Randall and noted that, though fewer than before, they were not gone.

Reports came also that Crow scouts had ridden with soldiers in other districts, offering knowledge of trails and camps in exchange for favor. The matter was spoken of without heat, yet it was not forgotten.

Mato asked his uncle one evening, "Will we fight?"

"Not now."

"Why?"

His uncle answered without haste. "We are not yet driven to it."

"Hunger decides?"

"Hunger," his uncle said, "and the closing of paths."

The wind pressed snow against the lodge walls that night, filling every small gap with cold.

The war in the East had thinned patrols. The war in Minnesota had shown how swiftly punishment could follow uprising. The United States could divide against itself and still assemble power enough to hang thirty-eight men in a single morning.

From this Mato drew a lesson.

The United States was not a single body that must stand whole or fall entire. It was many parts. Even when one part struck another, others continued their work.

He began to observe not only the fort but the patterns surrounding it.

Which patrols rode longer than before.

Which traders measured their words more carefully.

Which agents stiffened in manner when councils were called.

He was learning to measure more than movement.

He was learning to measure intention.

* * *

When spring returned, Dakota families were pressed westward. Reservation boundaries tightened. Agents spoke more firmly of compliance. Soldiers rode with clearer instruction.

Land contracted.

The Lakota watched. The Cheyenne listened. The lesson lay plain upon the ground:

When violence erupts, territory seldom expands.

One evening Mato stood above the Missouri and watched the thaw break the river ice into long grinding sheets.

"If they weaken," he asked his uncle, "is that our moment?"

"Perhaps," his uncle replied.

"And if they grow strong again?"

"Then we must be prepared for a strength greater than the one we knew."

Mato did not yet see how such preparation might be achieved. Yet he felt the necessity of it settle within him.

Once the United States had seemed a storm moving steadily westward.

Now he understood something further.

Storms may exhaust themselves.

But nations endure.

The Plains were no longer merely waiting.

They were taking measure.

And Mato Ska, standing at the edge of manhood, had begun to measure with them.

Chapter 3 -The Southern Wind

The first time Mato Ska heard the name Quanah Parker, it was spoken without boasting and without dismissal.

A trader had come north from the Red River country, his saddlebags scented with dust and mesquite rather than cottonwood and frost. His pony bore the marks of long travel through dry country. He had crossed grass that thinned into thorn and ridden where waterholes were known by memory rather than by map.

As he warmed his hands at the Lakota fire, he spoke of the southern Plains.

"The Comanche ride hard," he said. "Texas is thin now. Many of their soldiers have marched east. Ranches stand open."

The elders listened without interruption.

Mato listened closely.

He had begun to observe that tidings from the South arrived differently than those from the East. The East came folded in newspapers and carried in soldiers' mouths. The South came with men who had ridden far enough to taste two climates in one season.

"They strike Mexicans," the trader continued. "They strike Texans. They strike soldiers when soldiers appear. They take horses in number."

"Do they defeat the soldiers?" an elder asked.

The trader shifted his shoulders.

"They defeat the ones sent."

The distinction settled in Mato's mind.

The ones sent.

Not all.

* * *

The Plains did not share a single horizon.

Northward the Missouri bent broad and cold beneath the sky. Southward the land opened into heat and thorn, where wind carried dust instead of river scent. Yet stories traveled between these distances as readily as men.

Lakota riders spoke of Comanche horsemanship with respect. Cheyenne traders described raids that emptied ranch settlements in a single night. The Kiowa were said to strike without warning and vanish before pursuit gathered force.

Mato tried to imagine that southern country—harsher, without the river's steady line to guide the eye. He pictured riders who fought white soldiers as they hunted buffalo, with patience and sudden speed.

One evening he asked his uncle, "If the Comanche defeat soldiers, why do the soldiers keep coming?"

His uncle did not answer at once. He stirred the fire with a stick until sparks rose and settled.

"Because soldiers are not the whole of the white man," he said at last.

Mato frowned. "Then what is?"

His uncle drew a short line in the dirt.

"This is one rider," he said. "You knock him down. Another comes."

He drew another line beside it. Then another.

"And behind them?" Mato asked.

His uncle's hand moved again, extending the marks outward until they blurred in the fading light.

"More than we have yet seen."

* * *

As the war deepened in the East, the garrison at Fort Randall altered in temper. The buildings remained—the long barracks facing the parade ground, the storehouses, the flagstaff rising at the center. Yet the sound within the post changed.

Letters arrived more often than reinforcements. Officers spoke together in lowered voices. Some enlisted men declared openly that they wished to return east and fight nearer their homes.

Among the Lakota another word began to surface in council.

"If their attention is divided," one warrior said, "we press."

"Press where?" another asked.

Mato sat near the outer edge of the circle, listening.

"Where it costs them most," Red Cloud answered quietly.

The phrase remained with him.

Cost.

Not glory.

Not vengeance.

Cost.

* * *

More southern news came as the seasons turned.

Texas had joined the Confederacy. Southern officers now fought northern officers. Comanche bands rode into settlements left poorly defended.

Some Lakota allowed themselves a measure of satisfaction at the thought of white men turned upon one another.

Others were cautious.

"If the Confederates prevail," an elder asked, "do they return stronger?"

"And if they fail?" another replied.

"Then the Union returns stronger."

It was the first time Mato heard the distant war spoken of not merely as a white quarrel but as consequence for the Plains.

That evening he climbed the ridge above the river and looked southward, though he knew no eye could follow the land so far. He tried to imagine two white nations contending.

He wondered what would remain when one overcame the other.

* * *

One night a Cheyenne rider passed through the camp bearing a different account.

"They believe," the rider said, "that if they defeat the soldiers sent west, they defeat the white man."

The elders did not laugh.

Mato leaned forward. "Is that not so?"

The rider regarded him for a moment.

"How many soldiers have you seen in Washington City?" he asked.

"I have not seen Washington City."

"Few of us have."

The rider's gaze rested upon the fire.

"I have heard of buildings taller than any lodge," he said. "Of long streets filled with men in uniform. Of ships upon the great water that carry guns louder than thunder."

The circle grew still.

Mato understood then that the soldiers at Fort Randall were not the whole of what advanced across the continent. They were a portion only—visible, immediate, but not complete.

"If we strike the portion," he said slowly, "does the rest feel it?"

Red Cloud turned toward him.

"Yes."

"And does it bleed?"

A pause.

"Yes," Red Cloud said. "But not as a man bleeds. More slowly."

* * *

The name Quanah arose again in late autumn.

A young Comanche leader, the trader said. Half white by birth, wholly Comanche in allegiance. A fierce rider, yet one who watched before moving.

"He observes," the trader said. "He does not waste men."

The description fixed itself in Mato's mind—not because of the man's mixed blood, but because of that habit of watching.

Mato, too, had begun to watch before speaking.

He asked his uncle, "Will we ever meet them?"

"The Comanche?" his uncle said.

"Yes."

"Perhaps."

"And if we do?"

His uncle's expression revealed little.

"Then we shall learn whether we share more than enemies."

* * *

By the winter of 1862, Mato understood something he had not grasped two years before.

The United States was not a single rider moving west.

It was many riders.

Strike one, and another followed.

Yet riders could be delayed. Supplies could be taken. Costs could be imposed.

He did not yet know how such measures might be made lasting. But he sensed that striking soldiers was not the same as confronting the nation that sent them.

From the South came dust and movement.

From the East came distraction and warning.

Between them the Plains lay vast and patient.

And Mato Ska, no longer merely listening for sound, had begun to weigh distance, number, and consequence.

Chapter 4 -The Arm That Reaches

The war in the East did not end swiftly.

Two harvests passed while blue and gray armies met and broke against one another beyond the Mississippi. Reports of vast battles came and went like storms whose thunder was heard but whose lightning could not be seen.

Yet even as the white armies struck at each other, the reach of the United States did not slacken entirely.

Mato learned that in the season when the Dakota were hanged.

Thirty-eight.

The number endured long after the scaffold had been taken down. It traveled westward not as rumor but as confirmation—carried by traders, repeated by soldiers, spoken quietly by men who had stood in the crowd at Mankato and watched the platform fall.

"They tried them in groups," a Yanktonai visitor said. "Many in a single day. Some scarcely understood what was said against them."

"And the president?" an elder asked.

"He read the names."

That detail settled heavily upon Mato.

A man in Washington City, hundreds of miles distant, reading a list of Dakota men and deciding which would live and which would die.

"How can his voice reach so far?" Mato asked.

An elder beside him answered, "Because his power travels where his shadow does not."

Mato carried that thought with him.

Power without presence.

It was something he had not fully considered before.

* * *

When spring returned, Dakota families were driven westward under guard. Columns moved slowly across open country, soldiers riding alongside and behind. The Lakota watched from a distance as they passed.

They saw gaunt faces and bundles tied in haste. They saw children carried when their feet failed them. Blankets were drawn tight against a wind that did not soften for grief.

No one in Mato's camp spoke with satisfaction.

The lesson required no explanation.

When violence erupted, land diminished.

Reservation lines were spoken of more frequently in trader speech.

"It is for their protection," some agents said.

"It is to confine them," Mato's uncle replied quietly.

Mato asked, "If they draw lines upon the land, must we remain within them?"

His uncle regarded him steadily.

"If we cannot push those lines back, we remain where we are pressed."

The answer did not rest easily with him.

* * *

That summer word came that the Confederacy was weakening. Union armies advanced through the South. Rail lines in the East carried soldiers in number, day after day, like a river bearing driftwood in flood.

The image held Mato's attention.

He climbed again to the ridge above Fort Randall and looked upon the post with altered sight.

The long barracks still faced the parade ground. The flag still moved above the roofs. Supply wagons continued to arrive along the river road. Telegraph wires ran eastward, thin and nearly invisible against the sky.

The fort was not a wall.

It was a joining place.

Wagons came. Orders came. Patrols rode outward in steady measure.

If a wagon failed to arrive, what followed?

If the road were troubled, what then?

He began to watch not merely the soldiers but the movement that sustained them—the timing of deliveries, the intervals between patrols, the direction from which riders approached.

His uncle observed him.

"You study them as hunters study a herd," he said.

"They move in patterns," Mato answered.

"All men do."

"And patterns may be broken."

His uncle did not disagree.

* * *

Late in autumn news came from Colorado Territory.

It was brought by Cheyenne riders whose expressions bore neither fury nor surprise, but something more difficult to meet.

They had camped along Sand Creek Massacre beneath assurances of safety. An American flag had been raised above the lodges, and beneath it a white flag of truce.

"They said we would not be harmed," one Cheyenne elder said in council. "We believed them."

Soldiers came at dawn.

The account was given without raised voice. That restraint gave it weight.

Women running.

Children hiding along the creek bed.

Gunfire that did not cease when resistance failed.

"They carried their own flag above us," the elder said. "It did not prevent the killing."

Silence followed, deep and unbroken.

Mato felt something within him alter.

Trust, once extended, could be turned against the one who offered it.

* * *

That night he lay wakeful.

The United States fought itself in the East.

It hanged Dakota in Minnesota.

It struck Cheyenne who had gathered beneath a promise of safety.

Its reach extended even when it bled.

"How many arms does it have?" Mato asked his uncle the next morning.

"As many as it requires," his uncle replied.

The answer was not spoken harshly. It did not need to be.

* * *

In the weeks that followed, Lakota councils grew more deliberate.

Men spoke less of single raids and more of routes.

Less of counting coup and more of movement across country.

The Bozeman Trail was mentioned with increasing frequency—the road pushing northward through Powder River country toward the gold fields of Montana.

"They lay roads where they intend to remain," Red Cloud said.

"And raise posts where roads must be guarded," another added.

Mato listened.

"Then the road is what feeds them," he said carefully.

Several men turned toward him.

Red Cloud regarded him without dismissal.

"Yes."

"And if what feeds them is cut," Mato continued, "the post weakens."

The fire shifted, sending sparks upward.

No one laughed.

The thought required no embellishment.

***

Mato began to perceive a pattern that troubled him.

The Comanche struck soldiers in the South.

The Dakota rose and were punished.

The Cheyenne trusted and were destroyed.

Each suffered in its own country.

He waited until only a few men remained by the fire before speaking what lay upon his mind.

"If they strike Dakota alone," he said, "and Cheyenne alone, and Comanche alone… how long before they strike us alone?"

No one answered.

The answer lay already between them.

***

Snow returned early that year.

Mato sat beside the keeper of the winter count while the old man prepared to mark the hide.

"What image shall carry this season?" the elder asked.

Mato considered.

He thought of a flag above a creek. Of a scaffold raised in winter. Of roads pressed across hunting ground.

"Draw a road," he said at last.

The elder looked at him.

"Why a road?"

"Because it brings them," Mato replied.

"And if the road is troubled?"

"Then they must labor to keep it open."

The elder nodded and began his careful strokes.

Mato watched the image take shape.

He understood now that remembering was not solely for honoring what had passed.

It was instruction.

The war in the East moved toward its conclusion.

The reckoning upon the Plains had only begun.

And Mato Ska no longer listened merely for sound.

He watched for connection.

Chapter 5 - Powder River Country

1866

Powder River country did not yield itself easily to strangers. From a distance it appeared open and almost gentle—broad swells of grass rising and falling beneath a wide sky, pine-dark ridges standing at intervals, streams cutting narrow courses that turned sudden and treacherous after rain. There was no scent of great river there, no steady breath of the Missouri. The wind carried dust and the dry warmth of sun upon earth.

Mato had heard the country described in many councils.

He did not see it with his own eyes until he rode north in the spring of 1866.

They departed the Missouri while ice still clung to shaded banks and the ground, though softening, held the memory of frost. The column moved in measured order. Scouts ranged ahead and fell back again. Others trailed at distance.

This was no hunt.

It was examination.

Red Cloud rode near the center, neither pressing forward nor lingering behind. He spoke little while traveling. When he did, it was with economy.

"Count the wagons."

"Mark where timber has been cut."

"See where they water their horses."

The instructions were plain.

Mato rode among younger men, carrying more than he once would have been entrusted with—a rifle across his saddle, powder horn at his side, dried meat bound in hide. He spoke only when required.

The land demanded attention.

On the third day they crested a long rise and saw it.

The Bozeman Trail.

It did not appear formidable. A churned scar through grassland, wagon ruts hardened by repetition. Here and there timber had been felled to widen the path. Hoofprints overlapped in thickened earth.

"This is the road?" Mato asked quietly.

An older warrior beside him inclined his head.

"This is the road that feeds the posts."

They rode on.

Fort Reno stood first, timber buildings enclosed by a stout stockade, smoke lifting above the walls. A flag moved in the wind.

Farther north, Fort Phil Kearny rose near pine-covered ridges.

Beyond that, Fort C. F. Smith guarded the upper reaches.

Three wooden enclosures where none had stood before.

Red Cloud studied them from a distance.

"They are not built for passing through," he said to the gathered leaders. "They are built for remaining."

Mato understood.

A patrol camp could vanish with a season.

A fort required roads, timber, supply, protection.

It bound the land to what followed.

* * *

That evening Crazy Horse joined them.

Mato had seen him before across council circles—lean, self-contained, seldom eager to speak. In Powder River country he seemed fitted to the land, as though cut from its sharp lines.

He spoke without flourish.

"They believe the road is theirs because they travel it," he said. "Then we make it costly to travel."

No boast followed the words.

Mato watched the exchange between Red Cloud and Crazy Horse with care.

Red Cloud considered structure—roads, posts, seasons.

Crazy Horse considered motion—timing, distance, suddenness.

Together their thoughts aligned.

* * *

The first action was not grand.

A wagon bearing lumber and flour departed Fort Phil Kearny under light escort. Lakota and Cheyenne riders observed it from a distance, keeping to ridges and folds of land until the moment was chosen.

Mato rode with those assigned to flank.

His pulse beat hard in his throat.

This was not a raid for horses.

There would be no reckless charge.

They waited.

When the wagon descended into a narrow ravine, riders closed from ahead and behind. Gunfire sounded sharp and brief. Two soldiers fell. The remaining men broke toward the fort, abandoning their charge.

The wagon was set aflame.

Flour sacks burst in the heat, white dust rising into the wind like pale smoke.

Mato stood breathing hard, watching the wheels collapse inward.

"That is all?" he asked under his breath.

Red Cloud heard him.

"That is enough."

"We have not taken the fort."

"We need not take it," Red Cloud replied. "We must make it depend upon what it cannot safely gather."

The meaning settled slowly.

Hunger was not only of the belly.

* * *

In the weeks that followed, the pattern persisted.

Woodcutting parties were harried at the edge of the pine ridges. Patrols were drawn beyond the range of their guns. Smoke signals were raised to mislead. Telegraph wire was severed in short stretches and left for repair, then cut again.

The forts did not fall.

They strained.

Mato began to perceive the difference between defeating men and wearying what sustained them.

After one skirmish in which several soldiers lay dead and no Lakota were lost, Mato approached Crazy Horse.

"They return," Mato said. "Even when they lose men."

"Yes."

"Why?"

Crazy Horse regarded him steadily.

"Because they believe themselves large."

"And are they?"

"They are larger than what stands before us."

Mato thought of distant cities spoken of by traders—long streets and factories, ships upon waters beyond imagining.

"Then why can we press them here?" he asked.

"Because large bodies move with weight," Crazy Horse said.

"Weight slows."

The thought remained with Mato.

* * *

Winter approached early.

Snow complicated every movement. Supply trains required heavier escort. Woodcutting became perilous labor. Smoke rose from within the posts more frequently, as though warmth must be summoned in greater measure.

Then came the morning upon Lodge Trail Ridge.

Mato did not ride among those chosen to draw pursuit. He remained upon a secondary height and watched.

Captain William J. Fetterman led eighty men from Fort Phil Kearny in response to provocation. A small party of Lakota riders—Crazy Horse among them—allowed themselves to be seen and then withdrew, measured and deliberate.

The soldiers crossed beyond the ridge line, out of sight of their post.

Beyond sight lay numbers waiting.

The engagement was swift. It did not endure long enough for confusion to deepen into chaos. When it ended, no soldier remained standing.

Mato stood without movement.

He had seen skirmishes before.

He had not seen such finality.

There was no shouting when the warriors returned. No exultation.

Red Cloud spoke in low tones to those assembled.

"This does not end the matter," he said. "It alters it."

That night, beside a smaller fire, Mato asked his uncle, "What has changed?"

"We have shown them that the road costs more than they expected," his uncle replied.

"And will they leave?"

"They may reconsider."

Mato looked toward the darkness where the fort lay beyond sight.

The United States had not been broken.

But it had been compelled to answer.

* * *

Mato did not see Washington City or hear the debates that followed. He saw instead the smoke rising from posts forced into caution. He saw supply wagons travel under heavier guard. He saw hesitation where confidence had once seemed fixed.

For the first time he understood something clearly.

The United States might not be overcome in a single blow.

Yet it could be pressed.

Pressed where it fed itself.

Powder River country did not feel conquered.

It felt contested.

And Mato Ska, no longer merely watching from ridges above distant forts, had ridden within the contest and learned where weight might be applied.

Chapter 6 - Winter Council

The snow came in layers that year.

Not in a single storm that remade the land at once, but in patient coverings. A light fall settled into the grass. Days of wind pressed it thin across the ridges. Another storm softened the hills and filled the old wagon ruts until they vanished. By the time Mato Ska rode north toward the meeting place, the country lay muffled, as though sound itself had been weighed down.

He rode with two older warriors and spoke little.

He was trusted now with winter travel. He was not yet called upon to decide its purpose.

Powder River country lay still beneath the pale sky. The buffalo had drifted south earlier than many expected. That fact was not spoken of with alarm. It was noted and carried.

No runner announced the gathering.

No smoke signaled alliance.

Yet riders moved in wide arcs that bent toward a common ground.

Lakota came first.

Cheyenne emerged from the white sweep of prairie as though rising from it.

Arapaho riders arrived last, their approach quiet until their horses stood among the others.

The fires were built apart.

Not from hostility.

From habit.

Mato carried water between circles and listened.

He had witnessed councils before—disputes over grazing ground, over horses taken, over blood owed. He had never seen one so restrained.

Red Cloud arrived without ceremony. He dismounted, brushed snow from his shoulders, and stepped into the Lakota circle. Men shifted to make room. He did not raise his voice.

"The trail grows," he said.

None asked which trail.

The Bozeman Trail pressed through Powder River country toward the Montana gold fields. First had come wagons. Then surveyors. Then soldiers. Then timber cut for walls and roofs.

Fort Reno.

Fort Phil Kearny.

Fort C. F. Smith.

Posts were not passing camps.

They were declarations.

Across the distance, Little Wolf sat with his hands folded in his sleeves. Sand Creek Massacre lived in the set of his shoulders. He did not recount it. He did not need to.

"They spoke of protection," he said at length. "They raised their flag above us. They came at dawn."

Snow shifted beyond the circle in a slow wind.

Red Cloud inclined his head once.

"Then we do not stand beneath their flags again."

It was not spoken loudly.

It was accepted.

* * *

That night Mato crossed from one fire to another, returning a kettle and lingering at the edge of Cheyenne talk.

Old grievances had not dissolved. Lakota remembered horses taken in other winters. Cheyenne remembered ambushes along creek beds. Arapaho remembered both.

Yet something had altered since Sand Creek.

"They hang Dakota while fighting their own war," a Cheyenne elder murmured. "They kill us under promise. And still they build."

A Lakota warrior replied, "They divide us and strike where we stand alone."

The elder answered quietly, "Then we must not stand alone."

The words carried farther than raised voices.

* * *

On the second day Spotted Tail spoke.

"We must measure what we face," he said. "They fight among themselves and still they reach here. That means their strength is not easily broken."

Crazy Horse sat near the edge of the circle; eyes turned beyond the firelight.

"An arm may be broken," he said.

Spotted Tail did not contradict him, yet he did not yield.

"If you strike the hand and the body remains, what then?"

The tension between them was not anger.

It was difference.

Crazy Horse trusted the field.

Spotted Tail considered endurance beyond the field.

Red Cloud weighed position.

Mato watched and understood that they were not debating courage.

They were debating time.

* * *

On the third night, when many had withdrawn to rest and the fires burned low, Mato found himself near Red Cloud.

He had not intended to speak, yet the question rose.

"If the soldiers at the posts are defeated," he asked quietly, "will the road cease?"

Red Cloud studied him.

"They believe that if they send enough men, the land becomes theirs," he said. "We must teach them that the land asks more than they wish to give."

"By killing them?"

"By making them labor without gain."

The idea settled slowly.

Not conquest.

Burden.

* * *

On the fourth day a Cheyenne trader brought word from the South.

"The men who fight Washington are losing ground," he said carefully. "The Union armies push them back."

A low murmur passed through the circle.

Spotted Tail spoke first.

"If Washington wins, what follows?"

The trader answered without haste.

"Then it will no longer spend its strength upon its own war."

No one needed further explanation.

"All of it may turn west," an Arapaho elder said quietly.

Crazy Horse's voice cut through the stillness.

"Then we have little time."

Red Cloud regarded the fire before speaking.

"Or we have a narrow time. While they finish their struggle, their arm is divided. When it is no longer divided, it will reach farther."

Spotted Tail frowned.

"And if the South were to weaken Washington longer?"

"They cannot reach us," the trader replied. "Their fight is not for this land. But their resistance delays the one who is."

That settled the matter.

The war in the East was not opportunity in itself.

It was a clock.

Later that evening an Arapaho elder spoke of a journey east made by southern relatives.

"They saw Washington," he said.

Mato leaned forward.

"What did they see?"

"More soldiers than we have faced together. Buildings larger than any post. Guns in number. Rails that carry men without horses."

The circle shifted.

"So, we strike portions of something larger," Crazy Horse said.

"Yes."

Spotted Tail inclined his head.

"Then we must strike in ways that do not waste us."

Isolation had been named.

* * *

By the final morning no oath had been sworn. No banner lifted.

Yet the fires, once spaced apart, burned nearer than before. Smoke drifted together and mingled in the pale air.

"The posts along the Bozeman Road are not the heart," Red Cloud said. "They are veins."

He gestured westward.

"If the road fails, the posts cannot stand."

"We strike patrols," Crazy Horse said. "We trouble supply. We do not throw men against timber."

"If we succeed," Spotted Tail warned, "they will answer."

"Then we make the answer costly," Red Cloud replied.

Little Wolf spoke last.

"For the Cheyenne, Powder River is life."

"For the Lakota," Red Cloud answered, "it is the same."

The word alliance was not spoken.

It did not need to be.

* * *

As riders departed in staggered directions, leaving no single trail for pursuit, Mato lingered beside embers nearly hidden beneath snow.

Upon a narrow strip of hide he carried, he marked three small fires set close enough that their smoke touched.

Dakota had fought and been crushed in isolation.

Cheyenne had trusted and been betrayed in isolation.

Comanche fought in the south, far from this gathering.

Alone brought contraction.

Together brought risk.

But also, weight.

For the first time Mato had seen leaders of different nations speak not as rivals guarding separate ground, but as men considering a shared horizon.

He mounted and rode south with the Lakota band.

Snow erased their tracks quickly.

The land appeared unchanged.

Yet something had shifted.

Not uprising.

Not open war.

Design.

And design, Mato sensed, endured longer than anger.

Chapter 7 - Smoke on the Ridges

1867–1868

The snow that followed Lodge Trail Ridge lay undisturbed for days.

Word traveled faster than riders. By the time Mato returned to the outer ridges above Fort Phil Kearny, the post had altered in posture. Sentries stood doubled. Woodcutting parties no longer moved without heavy escort. Patrols rode tight and close, rarely straying beyond cannon sight.

The field beyond the ridge remained quiet.

No Lakota rider boasted of what had occurred there.

The soldiers had crossed beyond sight of their fort and had not returned.

That was sufficient.

* * *

The winter of 1867 tightened both sides.

The Army answered not with retreat but with reinforcement—more wagons, more men, heavier columns, and orders written in sharper tone.

Yet each reinforcement required supply.

Each supply required passage.

The Bozeman Trail, once a corridor of steady traffic, became cautious and strained. Wagons bunched together. Escorts rode thicker. Progress slowed to a crawl in deep snow.

Slowness was cost.

Mato lay again upon a ridge and counted.

Where once ten wagons passed in a morning, now four crept forward under doubled guard. Where woodcutters once ventured two miles beyond the walls, now they dared scarcely half that distance.

The forts stood.

But they no longer expanded.

* * *

Through spring and summer, the pattern hardened.

Lakota, Cheyenne, and Arapaho riders did not seek open battle. They cut telegraph wire in brief stretches. They drove off livestock. They struck small detachments and vanished into folds of land they knew intimately.

The Army adapted.

Scouts were hired from Crow country. Columns moved with greater caution. Officers learned not to pursue beyond ridge lines without support.

Mato saw something else emerging.

The war had become calculation on both sides.

Fewer reckless pursuits. Fewer unnecessary losses.

More waiting.

More watching.

Red Cloud spoke plainly one evening.

"They do not wish another Lodge Trail."

The name had already settled into speech.

"Then we deny them comfort," Crazy Horse answered.

No grand assault followed.

Instead came attrition.

* * *

By late 1867 the strain showed plainly.

Timber near the forts was exhausted. Woodcutting required long marches under guard. Hunting grew difficult under pressure. Horses weakened from constant readiness.

Among the Lakota the cost accumulated as well.

Hunters missed herds while shadowing patrols. Families moved often. Supplies thinned during hard months.

Victory, Mato learned, demanded endurance greater than anger.

* * *

News from the East confirmed what had long been expected.

The American Civil War had ended.

The southern armies were broken.

Washington no longer fought itself.

The arm that had been divided was whole again.

In council the meaning was understood without alarm.

Spotted Tail spoke first.

"They will not abandon this easily now."

"No," Red Cloud agreed. "But they must weigh what it costs to remain."

The question was no longer whether the Army could send more men.

It was whether the land would permit them to succeed.

* * *

Negotiations began quietly in 1868.

Envoys rode between posts and agencies. Promises were spoken of peace if the road were closed. Rumors passed through camps that the forts might be abandoned.

Few believed it at first.

Forts were anchors.

Anchors were not easily lifted.

Then smoke rose.

From a distant ridge Mato watched soldiers dismantle Fort Phil Kearny. What timber could not be removed was burned. Flames climbed into a sky once marked by the flag.

Fort Reno followed.

Fort C. F. Smith was emptied.

The Bozeman Trail fell silent.

No cheer rose from the watching riders.

Only a long breath.

They had not stormed the walls.

They had not seized the guns.

They had made the road too costly.

* * *

The Fort Laramie Treaty of 1868 recognized the Great Sioux Reservation and affirmed hunting rights in Powder River country.

On paper it appeared concession.

On the land it felt like proof.

The United States had been compelled to withdraw.

For the first time in Mato's life, he had seen the Army abandon forts under pressure from coordinated resistance.

Pride came quietly.

They had learned to fight not for spectacle but for effect.

They had learned to think in lines rather than circles.

Yet unease settled beneath that pride.

Reservation lines were drawn.

Recognition carried measurement.

Measurement carried limits.

* * *

Late that summer Mato rode alone across Powder River country.

No fort smoke marked the ridges now. Grass bent freely in the wind. The trail remained visible, but it fed nothing.

He understood something clearly.

They had won a contest of will.

They had proven that the United States could be made to reconsider.

But the United States still existed.

Whole again.

Stronger than when divided.

The next struggle would not come from thin patrols and distracted officers.

It would come from a government no longer at war with itself.

Mato turned his horse southward.

Victory had taught them coordination.

It had also announced their strength to Washington.

The land lay open once more.

For now.

And Mato Ska carried both triumph and warning within him as he rode home.

Chapter 8 - The Lines Drawn

1868–1871

When the Bozeman forts burned, Washington called it settlement.

Reports traveled east describing the Fort Laramie Treaty of 1868 as resolution. Powder River country recognized. A Great Sioux Reservation established. Peace secured.

Ulysses S. Grant spoke of a new direction—fewer open campaigns, more agents, more schools, more measured governance. In the capital it appeared orderly. Lines had been drawn. Territory defined.

The volatile West, once troublesome, seemed contained within ink.

On the Plains, the word peace did not settle so easily.

Mato rode south from Powder River country in the first summer after the treaty, not as a warrior but as a messenger. At first the land seemed unchanged—the same long grass bending under wind, the same creeks tracing patient curves through the earth.

Yet travel carried a different tension.

He passed boundary markers newly driven into soil that had never before required naming. The posts stood plain and unguarded, simple timber rising from grass.

He dismounted at one and laid a hand against it.

The wood did not resist him.

Yet the meaning of it did.

* * *

Farther south he encountered the first agency wagons.

Barrels of flour. Salt pork. Farming tools.

Missionaries rode beside government agents who spoke of instruction and settlement—of fields planted in rows and houses that did not move with the seasons.

Some families approached the ration lines cautiously, weighing winter against pride.

Others remained distant, unwilling to measure survival by allotment.

The buffalo did not recognize the treaty.

That autumn Mato rode west of Powder River with hunters, beyond where the boundary existed only on paper. The herds were smaller than the year before—not gone, but restless, shifting their movements farther each season.

They encountered the hunters soon enough.

These were not soldiers.

They were civilians with heavy rifles and wagons built for hides. Carcasses lay where they fell—tongues removed, hides stripped, the remainder abandoned to sun and scavenger.

Mato had seen men fall in battle.

This was something else.

Waste carried its own violence.

At the agencies officials spoke of regulation and licenses. Yet the wagons continued to arrive. Rail lines pushed westward. Cattle drives advanced north from Texas, longhorn herds trampling grass once crossed by buffalo.

Peace in treaty language did not bring stillness to the land.

* * *

At Fort Laramie, Red Cloud had refused to sign until the Bozeman forts were abandoned.

When the fires rose from their timbers, he placed his name upon the treaty.

Mato had watched that moment from a distance—white commissioners wiping sweat from their collars, satisfied expressions passing between them.

Crazy Horse did not sign.

He stood apart during the negotiations and listened without offering commitment. When the papers were sealed and the commissioners rode east, he gathered with several leaders along the riverbank.

"You draw a line," he said, tracing one into the earth with a stick, "and soon you live inside it."

Some answered that the boundary brought time—fewer soldiers along Powder River, fewer patrols crossing hunting ground.

Crazy Horse pressed the stick deeper.

"If the buffalo cross the line, do we stop following?"

No one replied.

"If miners cross the line, does Washington stop them?"

Silence remained.

Mato watched him closely. This was not defiance spoken in anger. It was refusal to accept that land could be contained without consequence.

The distinction troubled Mato more than open war.

* * *

Pressure in the south grew stronger rather than weaker.

In 1870 Mato rode there with a small delegation, traveling many days through country that felt both familiar and changed. Rivers ran low that summer, forcing long detours. Watch was kept even in places where peace was said to exist.

Texas ranching had expanded quickly. Fences crept outward. Buffalo hunters traveled in greater numbers. Their camps carried the sour scent of hides curing beneath the sun.

Rail surveys crossed Kansas and moved toward Indian Territory, thin lines of iron promising permanence.

Quanah Parker met them in a shallow valley ringed with mesquite.

He was younger than many northern leaders, yet his gaze carried careful attention.

"You forced them to abandon the forts," he said.

"It cost them to remain," Mato answered.

Quanah considered the words.

"In the south," he said slowly, "they believe the cost can be paid."

He spoke of herds thinning faster each season. Of southern Cheyenne bands confined more tightly. Of Kiowa riders pushed from hunting ground by ranchers who carried documents and soldiers to enforce them.

"The Army has changed," Quanah added. "They are not fighting their own war now."

There was no admiration in the observation.

Only understanding.

The United States had learned from Powder River.

It had adjusted.

* * *

In Washington attention moved elsewhere.

Reconstruction in the South demanded political effort. Railroad companies pressed for land grants and protection. Investors spoke of the West as open ground waiting for settlement.

Indian agents reported progress.

Reservation schools were described as success.

From such distance the Plains appeared manageable.

Contained.

Yet across that wide country leaders were studying the same pattern.

In 1871 a Kiowa intermediary rode north under the pretense of trade. He remained quiet through much of the council, speaking only after long listening.

"What did it require," he asked finally, "to make them abandon the forts?"

Red Cloud answered without embellishment.

"Cost."

Crazy Horse added, "Patience."

Little Wolf spoke one word.

"Unity."

The Kiowa rider carried that word south with him.

Unity.

It did not spread loudly.

But it did not disappear.

* * *

That winter Mato attended a gathering larger than any he had previously seen.

Lakota. Northern Cheyenne. Arapaho. Kiowa envoys. Comanche observers.

The camps were arranged apart, yet the fires stood near enough that their smoke mingled before rising.

Travel to the council had taken him nearly two weeks. Snow lay uneven across the plains, horses tiring quickly in drifts. Progress was measured in careful miles rather than swift rides.

The discussion did not concern a single road.

It concerned pattern.

"They believe we now live within their lines," Crazy Horse said.

"They believe we accepted their peace," Red Cloud answered.

A Comanche envoy spoke carefully.

"In the south there is no peace."

Spotted Tail added a harder truth.

"If we fight again, they will say we break the treaty."

Crazy Horse looked slowly around the circle.

"Did all of us agree to that treaty?"

Silence settled heavily.

Not every band had signed. Not every leader had consented.

The treaty was not universal.

Its authority therefore could not be universal.

Mato felt the shift before anyone spoke it plainly.

They were no longer debating whether resistance might return.

They were considering how resistance could move across distance.

Men traced supply routes into the snow with gloved fingers. They spoke of telegraph lines and river traffic. They counted garrisons and studied the rhythm of rations delivered to distant posts.

They discussed preserving buffalo not only as sustenance, but as strategy.

Without herds there was no mobility.

Without mobility there was no war.

They were no longer reacting.

They were studying.

* * *

President Grant believed his Peace Policy had steadied the frontier.

Rail construction accelerated. Cattle drives lengthened. Speculators described the Plains as territory open for business.

Few in Washington imagined that the tribes of the Plains were beginning to think beyond local defense.

That misjudgment deepened quietly.

One evening, when the council fires had burned low and conversation thinned to murmurs, Mato stepped beyond the circle and looked across the dark prairie.

Smoke rose in layered columns and mingled before dissolving into the night.

He felt pride in what had been achieved—the forts abandoned, the treaty forced upon their terms.

Yet beneath the pride lay unease.

Lines had been drawn.

Washington believed the matter settled.

Belief could be as dangerous as ignorance.

Mato understood now that endurance alone would not suffice.

Design required foresight.

Pressure had once been placed upon a single road and had moved an army.

What might happen if pressure were placed upon many roads at once?

The thought did not excite him.

It steadied him.

The Plains were quiet that night.

Not from surrender.

From calculation.

Chapter 9 - The Hills and the Breaking of Peace

1874–1876

By 1874 many in Washington believed the Plains question had been resolved.

The Fort Laramie Treaty of 1868 had drawn its boundaries. The Great Sioux Reservation had been marked upon government maps. Powder River country remained hunting ground. The Black Hills lay within the reservation itself.

On paper the land belonged to the Lakota.

The Lakota did not call the region the Black Hills.

They called it Paha Sapa.

The heart of everything that is.

* * *

Mato had first entered the Hills as a boy.

He remembered the moment when prairie grass yielded to rising stone and dark pine timber, how the air cooled beneath the forest canopy as though one had stepped through a doorway. Sound carried differently there. Wind softened. Hoofbeats sank into the floor of needles and moss.

Men traveled to Paha Sapa seeking visions. Ceremonies began among those ridges. Streams did not simply run—they carried memory.

Hunting ground could be measured.

Origin could not.

In the years after the Bozeman forts burned, Mato returned often to the Hills—not to hide nor prepare for war, but to listen. The forest quieted a man's thinking. Sunlight filtered through branches in narrow shafts. Granite ridges stood patient and unmoved.

Peace seemed to hold.

Agencies distributed rations. Some bands moved nearer the reservation lines, balancing winter survival against independence. Others remained beyond them, unwilling to bind their movements to ink.

Yet rumors began drifting across the Plains.

Gold.

* * *

Miners had whispered of it for years.

Flecks in creek gravel. Color caught in streambeds. Traders repeated the stories. Investors listened carefully. After the financial panic of 1873 the United States searched anxiously for stability.

Gold promised certainty.

Gold promised expansion.

Officially the Hills were protected by treaty.

Unofficially pressure gathered.

In the summer of 1874 Lieutenant Colonel George Armstrong Custer led a large column of cavalry, engineers, and surveyors into Paha Sapa. The expedition was described as reconnaissance—an exploration to map the region and examine its resources.

Miners followed the soldiers.

They carried pans.

That detail traveled faster than any official dispatch.

* * *

Among those watching the column from distant ridges was an Arikara leader called One Stab.

He was not part of the soldiers' command.

He shadowed them.

From pine-covered slopes he counted men, wagons, and horses. He watched how cavalry patrols spread outward and how often they returned. Soldiers unfamiliar with the Hills sometimes trusted the ground too easily.

One Stab did not.

Yet curiosity or caution brought him too near one afternoon along a narrow stream. Cavalry patrols cut him off before he could reach open ground.

He was taken before the officers.

"Why are you here?"

"I know these hills," he replied.

"Who sent you?"

"No one."

Suspicion lingered. Yet the expedition pressed deeper into country its maps poorly described. Wagons stalled where slopes steepened suddenly. Streams narrowed into stone cuts that trapped wheels.

One Stab offered advice sparingly.

"This pass will slow you."

"There is water beyond that ridge."

"If you turn south here, your wagons will hold."

Usefulness softened suspicion.

He remained long enough to see what mattered.

Miners drifted away from the column whenever streams appeared promising. They knelt in cold water and sifted gravel through their pans.

At first, they found nothing.

Then one day a fleck remained that did not wash away.

The tone of voices changed.

Gold lay in the Hills.

* * *

One Stab escaped during a night of steady rain.

By the time soldiers realized he was gone he had already vanished into timber and stone that knew him better than they did.

Days later he reached Lakota and Cheyenne camps.

"They bring miners behind the soldiers," he said. "They search the streams."

The council hardened.

Miners were not protection.

Miners were invasion.

* * *

At first the United States attempted to enforce its own treaty.

Army patrols rode into the Hills to drive miners away. Camps were dismantled. Wagons were burned. One group of prospectors—later known as the Gordon party—built a rough stockade beside a stream and began digging.

Soldiers removed them and burned their settlement.

For a moment Washington attempted to hold the line it had drawn.

But gold traveled faster than orders.

Each wagon forced out of the Hills was replaced by two more. Prospectors slipped through timber beyond the reach of patrols. Trails multiplied across valleys the Army could not easily watch.

The treaty still existed.

But it was becoming impossible to enforce.

* * *

In 1875 Washington attempted a different solution.

A scientific survey entered the Hills under geologist Walter P. Jenney. Among the men traveling with the expedition was physician Valentine McGillycuddy, who studied the terrain with instruments and notebooks rather than rifles.

Their purpose was to determine the truth about the rumored gold.

By the time their work concluded the secret had already escaped.

Their report confirmed what miners suspected.

Gold existed in the Black Hills.

Newspapers printed the word in large type.

After that the rush could not be stopped.

* * *

Washington attempted negotiation.

Commissioners approached Lakota leaders with offers of money, supplies, and expanded reservation lands in exchange for the Hills.

The answer was simple.

No.

Paha Sapa could not be sold.

The refusal frustrated officials who had already begun imagining the land opened to mining.

Public pressure grew. Railroad companies demanded access. Investors spoke openly of expansion.

Washington changed its strategy.

* * *

In the winter of 1875, the government issued a new order.

All Lakota bands living beyond reservation boundaries were required to report to the agencies by the end of January 1876. Any who remained in the hunting country after that date would be considered hostile.

The order was impossible.

Many bands were deep in winter hunting grounds. Some lived hundreds of miles away. Others never received the message at all.

But the deadline passed.

In Washington the conclusion was simple.

The Indians had refused.

The Army was ordered to act.

* * *

Three columns were sent into the northern Plains.

George Crook advanced north from Wyoming Territory.

John Gibbon moved east from Montana.

From Dakota Territory Alfred Terry marched west.

With Terry rode the Seventh Cavalry under Lieutenant Colonel George Armstrong Custer.

Their purpose was not negotiation.

They were to locate the villages that remained beyond the reservation and force them back inside it.

* * *

Across the Plains the response was measured rather than sudden.

The Hills had already shown that treaties could be broken when gold demanded it. The new order only confirmed what many leaders already believed.

Lakota, Cheyenne, and Arapaho bands continued their seasonal movements. Spring gave way to early summer. Buffalo herds drifted northward across the valleys of the Yellowstone and Little Bighorn.

Families followed the herds as they always had.

Villages gathered gradually.

Some came because hunting was good. Others came because soldiers were moving in several directions at once. Still others came simply because summer gatherings had long been part of Plains life.

Yet the encampment that formed along the Little Bighorn River grew larger than any in recent memory.

Lakota bands arrived first.

Northern Cheyenne joined them.

Arapaho families came soon after.

Tipis spread in long arcs beside the river, their numbers growing with each passing week.

It was not a war council.

It was a gathering of people who had chosen not to live inside the reservation lines.

* * *

Scouts rode far beyond the village.

They watched army patrols moving through distant valleys. Telegraph wires hummed along new routes across the Plains. Supply wagons moved between forts.

The soldiers were searching.

Mato rode into the great encampment after days of careful travel. The village stretched farther than he had ever seen. Smoke rose in layered columns above thousands of lodges.

Children played along the riverbank.

Hunters returned with buffalo.

Horses grazed in hidden coulees beyond the camp.

They had not gathered expecting annihilation.

They had gathered to live.

Yet everyone understood the soldiers were coming.

The Army believed it was enforcing law.

The Plains believed the law had already been broken.

Between those understandings rode the Seventh Cavalry.

And the land, as always, listened.

Chapter 10 - Greasy Grass

June 1876

They had not gathered for war.

That was what Mato would remember most clearly.

The village along the Greasy Grass pulsed with ordinary life. Children chased one another between the lodges. Women scraped hides and laughed at something overheard. Dogs barked at shadows and were scolded away. Horses grazed in long patient lines along the surrounding hills, their tails flicking lazily at flies.

The camp was immense—larger than any Mato had ever seen assembled in one place.

Lakota bands from across the northern Plains had arrived first. Northern Cheyenne joined them soon after. Arapaho families followed. Some had come to avoid the tightening pressure of the agencies. Some had come for the summer hunt. Others came simply because movement itself had become resistance.

Not united by proclamation.

United by pressure.

The scale of the village unsettled Mato at first. So many lodges meant so many decisions. So many young men eager to prove themselves. So many children who would pay dearly if caution failed.

Yet the camp was not careless.

Horse herds were arranged deliberately. Some grazed where distant observers could see them—enough to suggest strength, not enough to reveal scale. Others were concealed behind low ridges and in shallow draws, tended by boys who understood that visibility itself could be strategy.

Scouts rode wide arcs along the surrounding hills.

Nothing rigid.

Nothing theatrical.

They did not wait passively.

They watched.

* * *

George Armstrong Custer carried a reputation that had traveled across the Plains long before he did.

He moved quickly.

He divided his forces.

He believed speed and surprise could break a village before it gathered strength. More than once he had tried to seize women and children to force surrender.

The leaders of the camp spoke of this during the quiet hours of evening.

"This time," Gall said one night beside the fire, his voice steady, "they will not find us unaware."

* * *

Before Custer reached the valley, another column advanced from the south.

Dust appeared first along the distant horizon. Scouts returned with urgency but without panic.

General George Crook.

Crazy Horse rode south with a strong force of Lakota and Cheyenne warriors to meet him before his column could unite with the others moving across the Plains.

Mato rode partway with them, then turned back with a reserve nearer the Greasy Grass, where riders waited ready to move in either direction.

The fighting along the Rosebud River was sprawling and confused. No fixed lines. No single center. Riders surged forward, withdrew, then returned again through folds of broken ground.

Crook's soldiers fought stubbornly.

But by evening the column halted and withdrew southward.

Not destroyed.

But delayed.

When word returned to the Greasy Grass, no celebration followed.

The leaders simply understood what it meant.

Custer would not have Crook beside him.

* * *

Days later, more scouts arrived with urgent news.

Custer had divided his regiment.

The information moved quietly through the village, carried in low voices from lodge to lodge.

He believes we are fewer.

He believes speed will overwhelm us.

He believes this is another raid.

Mato felt the shift within himself as clearly as he felt the ground beneath his horse. For years, Plains leaders had studied the Army's habits—the way officers counted advantage, the way they relied upon surprise.

Now surprise belonged to the valley.

* * *

The attack came near midday.

Gunfire cracked along the southern edge of the village as Major Marcus Reno's battalion advanced toward the timber beside the river.

Dust and smoke tangled above the lodges.

The camp did not dissolve into blind panic.

It moved.

Women gathered children and hurried toward the wooded banks where the river cut steep channels. Older men urged them on. Boys drove horse herds toward concealed ravines beyond sight.

The sound was immense—shouting, hooves, rifles—but beneath it ran a current of intention.

Mato mounted without conscious thought.

Years of watching and riding had sharpened his instincts. He did not charge toward the first gunfire. He circled wide instead, reading the movement, seeking where the Army's momentum could be broken.

Reno's men faltered first.

They had expected the village to scatter.

Instead, riders appeared from every direction.

What had seemed a resting camp became a gathering force. Warriors who had been sleeping, hunting, or talking only moments earlier rode hard toward the timber.

Reno's formation began to unravel.

Under mounting pressure his men withdrew toward the bluffs, leaving their dead among the cottonwoods.

* * *

There was little pause.

From the north another column appeared.

Custer.

He rode toward what he believed would be weakness—lodges unguarded, families in flight, confusion to exploit.

Instead, he found resistance already forming.

Mato rode toward the northern ridges as warriors streamed past him in widening arcs. He saw Crazy Horse cutting across a shallow coulee, guiding riders not with shouted commands but with presence alone. He saw Gall rallying men along the riverbank.

Custer's battalion tried to hold higher ground.

The terrain betrayed them.

Ridges broke into ravines. Sightlines collapsed without warning. Commands vanished beneath wind and rifle fire.

Near a narrow stream cut, Mato saw cavalry attempting to regroup. He fired once, then again, aiming carefully rather than wildly. Around him riders pressed closer—some armed with rifles, others with bows or weapons taken in earlier fights.

There was no uniformity of arms.

Only convergence.

Custer's line faltered.

Horses screamed and fell. Soldiers dismounted and tried to form defensive clusters. Each moment the clusters shrank as riders closed from every direction.

Momentum shifted by degrees—one broken flank, one failed regrouping, one retreat to ground offering little shelter.

Then silence.

When the firing ended, every soldier of that northern battalion lay dead.

* * *

The field did not feel triumphant.

It felt heavy.

Warriors moved quickly across the ground. Weapons were gathered. Horses seized. Some riders pushed southward to increase pressure on the surviving soldiers under Reno and Benteen.

Behind them women walked the field where smoke drifted low.

Ritual began.

Not frenzy.

Not spectacle.

Spiritual conclusion.

Bodies were altered according to belief so enemies would not carry their full selves into the next world. Some soldiers were left untouched.

Custer's body was found among them.

He had not been mutilated.

Leadership—even in opposition—carried its own recognition.

* * *

By afternoon the meaning of the day settled across the valley.

More than two hundred soldiers lay dead.

Tribal losses were far fewer.

It was decisive.

It was also dangerous.

Mato rode along the ridge as evening fell and watched smoke drift slowly into the sky. He had seen forts burn. He had seen treaties signed. He had watched patterns bend.

This was different.

This was humiliation.

And humiliation demanded response.

* * *

Within hours the great village began to dissolve.

Lakota bands moved toward the Bighorn Mountains. Cheyenne drifted back toward Powder River country. Some prepared to move north beyond immediate reach.

The gathering that had created strength would become vulnerability if it lingered.

Plans were made to meet again.

Not here.

At Bear Butte.

Sacred ground.

There they would decide what must come next.

* * *

In Washington disbelief came first.

Reports were questioned. Numbers recalculated. Survivors' accounts examined for error.

Then outrage followed.

Newspapers called it massacre. Politicians demanded retaliation. Investors warned of instability across the frontier. Military leaders called for overwhelming force.

President Ulysses S. Grant listened carefully.

He understood something few wished to admit aloud.

This had not been a small frontier engagement.

It had become continental.

* * *

Days later Mato stood above the valley where the grass had begun to lift again.

The Little Bighorn flowed quietly between its banks as if nothing extraordinary had occurred.

He did not feel triumph.

He felt movement.

For the first time tribes across the Plains had acted in parallel at decisive scale. They had demonstrated not merely resistance, but capacity.

The question had changed.

No longer Can we win battles?

Now:

What follows victory?

Wind moved steadily across the Greasy Grass, bending the tall summer grass in long unified waves.

Mato watched it carefully.

This battle was not an ending.

It was an opening.

And openings, he understood now, could be more dangerous than defeat.

Chapter 11 - After the Victory

Summer–Autumn 1876

The camps did not travel together.

They never had.

Lakota bands moved in long arcs across the plains, following water and memory. Cheyenne drifted along river valleys their grandfathers had known. Arapaho riders appeared and disappeared like weather across the grass. Southern envoys came more slowly, wary of patrol routes and telegraph lines that now stitched the country together in thin threads of iron.

Yet though they traveled apart, they moved toward the same place.

Bear Butte.

The dark mass rose alone from the prairie, lifting steeply from the grasslands as though placed there deliberately. It did not sprawl like the Black Hills. It stood solitary against the sky, visible for many miles.

It had always been sacred.

Now it would carry something more.

* * *

The summer after Greasy Grass did not bring safety.

It brought consequence.

The vast encampment along the Little Bighorn dissolved within days of the battle. Lakota bands moved toward the Bighorn Mountains. Cheyenne drifted back toward Powder River country. Arapaho slipped quietly into lands they knew could shield them.

No one lingered long enough to invite the Army's return.

Word spread quickly that the United States would not accept humiliation quietly.

New columns were forming. Supply depots expanded along the railheads. River crossings filled with wagons and soldiers. Telegraph lines hummed with urgent messages moving east and west across the frontier.

Everyone understood what that meant.

Retaliation would not be small.

* * *

Sitting Bull made his decision early.

He would not wait to see where Washington struck first.

With the Hunkpapa and those who chose to follow him, he moved north toward the Medicine Line. The journey was deliberate rather than hurried. They traveled in stages, avoiding main patrol routes, conserving horses, crossing rivers where the current ran shallow.

Crossing into Canada was not flight.

It was repositioning.

North of that line the United States Army could not pursue freely without provoking the British authorities who governed the territory.

There Sitting Bull could preserve his people and watch what Washington chose to do next.

"He guards the north," Crazy Horse said when word of the move reached the other bands.

Washington would call it retreat.

On the Plains it was understood as strategy.

* * *

By the time Mato rode toward Bear Butte in late summer, Sitting Bull was already beyond American reach.

Mato rode west from the Missouri country, leaving the quiet watch near Fort Randall behind him. The journey required patience. Army patrols had multiplied across the plains, and the open country no longer belonged entirely to those who knew it best.

Once he circled widely around a column moving north along the White River valley. Another time he waited nearly half a day in broken badlands while a cavalry patrol crossed the open country ahead of him.

Telegraph crews now guarded the lines that ran toward the mining camps in the Black Hills, rifles resting across their knees as if the wire itself carried authority.

He saw no large encampments.

That was deliberate.

What had once gathered in one immense village now moved in fragments. Each band protected its own path, yet all angled toward the same horizon.

Bear Butte.

* * *

He reached the butte near dusk.

Smoke rose in steady columns along its base. Camps were arranged carefully—not crowded together, yet not scattered carelessly. Riders moved between them without urgency but with purpose.

No drums marked celebration.

No boasting carried across the grass.

Victory had brought gravity.

They had destroyed a regiment of the United States Army.

The response would reshape everything.

* * *

Red Cloud arrived with a modest escort, his expression controlled. Spotted Tail came later, thoughtful and reserved. Little Wolf stood near the outer fire ring, listening more than speaking.

Crazy Horse moved between camps without ceremony, speaking briefly with one group and then another, gathering news rather than offering it.

Southern envoys brought harder reports.

In Texas and Indian Territory, the Army had strengthened its forts. Buffalo herds were thinning rapidly beneath the rifles of hide hunters. Cattle now spread across country where buffalo had once moved freely. Rail surveys pushed steadily westward month by month.

Victory in the north had not eased pressure.

It had intensified it.

* * *

"We forced them from Powder River," Red Cloud said quietly that evening. "We defeated Custer. Yet they still come."

"They will not stop for gold," Spotted Tail replied.

"They did not stop for flags," Little Wolf added.

Crazy Horse stood in the firelight, shadows crossing his face.

"If we fight each place separately," he said, "we shrink separately."

No one spoke the word alliance.

It no longer needed to be spoken.

* * *

Mato sat near the outer edge of the council.

Once he had strained to follow such conversations. Now he recognized the pattern easily.

They spoke not of revenge.

They spoke of sequence.

Not of pride.

Of position.

Discussion turned to forts. Telegraph lines. Supply routes along the Missouri River. Places where pressure might be applied quietly rather than dramatically.

Red Cloud did not issue commands.

He asked questions.

"If one fort were to falter quietly," he said, "what would they believe?"

"They would blame their officers first," Spotted Tail answered.

"And if more than one?"

No one finished the thought.

They did not need to.

* * *

Beyond the councils another circle formed.

A messenger from the far West had arrived weeks earlier with word of a vision—a world renewed, buffalo returning in unbroken herds, ancestors walking again across the plains.

The story traveled by horse and memory, changing shape as it moved.

Among the Lakota and Cheyenne, it arrived not as command but as possibility.

Men and women joined hands.

No one announced the beginning.

Feet pressed slowly into the earth.

Step.

Draw.

Turn.

Breathe.

Mato stepped into the outer ring.

The hands beside him trembled—not from fear of soldiers, but from something deeper: fear that the world they had known would vanish before their children could know it fully.

The rhythm steadied.

Voices layered over one another.

The circle tightened, then widened again, like breath.

A young man collapsed near the center, trembling. Women knelt beside him as he spoke of visions—buffalo cresting distant ridges beyond counting, ancestors walking unharmed across the plains.

Some believed the vision would unfold exactly as spoken.

Others understood it differently.

It did not matter.

The strength lay not in prophecy.

It lay in unity.

* * *

For years they had answered pressure with strategy.

Now they answered fear with identity.

The dance was not preparation for battle.

It was preparation for endurance.

By the third night more circles formed. No council ordered it. No chief directed it. The movement spread quietly from camp to camp like wind through grass.

Warriors who had fought fiercely along the Greasy Grass now moved in measured rhythm. Mothers who had fled gunfire lifted their voices toward the night sky.

Mato felt something shift within himself.

He had watched grief become anger.

Anger become strategy.

Strategy become victory.

Now he watched belief become structure.

Shared ritual built shared resolve.

Resolve, once shared, resisted fracture.

* * *

Late that night Mato climbed a rise beneath Bear Butte and looked across the camps scattered beneath the stars.

No banner had been raised.

No declaration proclaimed.

Yet something irreversible had begun.

They were no longer aligning only in resistance.

They were aligning in spirit.

And spirit, Mato understood, could endure where armies could not.

Far to the east, new armies were already forming.

Winter would come soon enough.

And with it, the true measure of what victory had begun.

Chapter 12 - The Winter Campaign

1876–1877

Winter did not wait for permission on the northern plains.

It arrived first in wind that cut sharper each morning, then in snow settling along creek beds and north-facing slopes. By late November the land had hardened. Hoofprints froze overnight. Rivers narrowed beneath growing ice. The prairie that had carried so many riders through summer now held them carefully, measuring every mile.

For generations, war on the plains had followed the seasons.

Campaigns ended when winter came. Soldiers withdrew to their forts. Horses weakened in deep snow. Warriors returned to sheltered valleys where wood and water could be found.

That rhythm had protected the tribes as much as it protected the army.

Now the rhythm was breaking.

Mato began to understand this in the weeks after the camps dispersed from Greasy Grass.

He rode often that winter between scattered bands, carrying word where it was needed and listening where talk gathered. The great village that had filled the valley along the Little Bighorn was gone, dissolved into smaller movements across thousands of miles of open land. Each band traveled cautiously, choosing winter ground with care.

But soldiers were moving too.

Not waiting.

Moving.

* * *

The first reports came from the south.

Columns under General Crook had begun riding long before the spring grass returned. Infantry marched where horses failed, their breath thick in the freezing air. Wagons followed with supplies hauled across frozen ground that summer mud would have swallowed.

Villages that believed winter would protect them were surprised in their sleep.

Lodges burned quickly in dry wind. Pony herds were seized before they could scatter into broken country. Food stores that would have carried families through the cold months vanished in sudden flame.

The soldiers did not linger after the attacks.

They did not need to.

They left the winter itself to finish the work.

* * *

Other columns moved from different directions.

Along the Yellowstone, units under General Terry pushed westward in slow, relentless marches. Farther south, new patrols appeared along the Platte and the Powder River, watching crossings once used freely.

The army was no longer hunting a single village.

It was tightening the land.

Mato saw the change with his own eyes that January.

He rode west across country he had known since childhood, following a route that once carried buffalo herds in numbers that darkened entire ridges. Now the snow lay unbroken for long stretches. When tracks did appear, they were often mule prints left by supply trains or the narrow grooves of sled runners hauling military stores.

Near the Tongue River he found the charred remains of a camp that had stood there only weeks before.

Ash lay scattered across the snow where lodge poles had collapsed. Broken travois frames leaned against frozen cottonwoods. The wind had already begun to erase smaller signs of struggle, but deeper tracks remained—the marks of wagons that had hauled away captured supplies.

He dismounted and stood there for a long time without speaking.

This had not been battle.

It had been removal.

* * *

Word spread quickly through the winter camps.

Crook.

Miles.

Terry.

Names that had once belonged to distant reports now moved through conversation like approaching weather.

Some warriors argued that the soldiers could still be defeated in open battle.

They pointed to Greasy Grass.

Others were less certain.

Greasy Grass had been a moment when the army moved quickly and believed itself stronger than it was. Now the army moved differently—slowly, deliberately, in many directions at once.

Mato heard the difference in the way older men spoke.

They did not speak of courage.

They spoke of supply.

They spoke of horses.

They spoke of how long food might last when a band was forced to keep moving in deep snow.

The war was changing shape.

* * *

Late that winter Mato rode north toward Powder River country with two Cheyenne scouts who had passed through the region days earlier. The journey took longer than expected. Snow lay deeper along the valleys, and more than once they were forced to circle wide around patrols moving along the river bottoms.

On the third evening they reached a ridge overlooking a narrow basin where a village had once stood.

Only the poles remained.

The lodges had been cut down and burned. Meat caches that should have hung in nearby trees were gone. Even the smaller ponies that children rode had been taken.

One of the Cheyenne scouts knelt beside the frozen ground where a corral had once stood.

"They came before dawn," he said quietly.

Mato did not ask how he knew.

The sign was clear enough.

* * *

The soldiers had learned.

They no longer waited for the tribes to gather.

They attacked when the tribes were weakest.

They struck food first.

Horses second.

Shelter third.

It was not the kind of war Mato had grown up watching.

It was colder.

More patient.

More certain of its own time.

* * *

When Mato returned east in early spring he stopped for a night along a bluff overlooking the Missouri.

Far below, the river had begun to break apart again. Ice that had sealed it through winter drifted slowly downstream in long silent slabs. The current moved beneath them, steady and indifferent to what happened on the banks.

Forts still stood along that river.

Supply wagons still moved between them.

Telegraph lines carried messages that crossed half the continent faster than any horse could ride.

The soldiers had learned how to break villages in winter.

The tribes would have to learn something else.

Mato sat there until the light faded and the wind shifted across the frozen grass.

For years they had fought the army where the army appeared.

But the army was not only soldiers.

It was roads.

It was supplies.

It was wires that carried orders across the land.

If those things could be broken, the soldiers would not move so easily.

The thought settled slowly in his mind—not as anger, but as recognition.

By the time he rode south again, word had already begun to spread among the bands.

There were other ways to fight.

Bear Butte had been the place where that idea was first spoken aloud.

The winter campaign had shown why it would be necessary.

Somewhere along the Missouri, a fort still watched the frozen river and believed the war remained far away.

It did not yet understand that the war had changed.

Chapter 13 - Fort Randall

Winter did not loosen its grip quickly that year.

Even as the days lengthened, cold lingered along the Missouri. Snow lay in narrow drifts where the wind had piled it against bluffs and cottonwood groves. Ice still moved slowly along the river's center, breaking apart in dull grinding sheets that drifted south toward warmer country.

The land carried the marks of the winter campaign.

Villages burned.

Horse herds scattered or taken.

Food stores destroyed before spring could soften the ground.

For months the Army had moved across the Plains in ways the tribes had not expected. Soldiers rode when the snow was deepest and struck when camps believed themselves protected by season and distance.

The message had been clear.

The United States had learned.

Now the Plains leaders were learning in return.

* * *

Fort Randall stood above the Missouri as it had for nearly twenty years.

From a distance it appeared unchanged. Timber walls weathered gray by wind and sun. Barracks aligned in orderly rows. Officers' quarters set slightly apart from the enlisted buildings. Smoke rose from chimneys in steady lines, carrying the smell of coal and wood downriver.

To Washington, it was a mark on a map.

To the Yanktonai, it was a pattern.

And patterns, once understood, become vulnerable.

They had watched the fort for years.

Not as an enemy to be charged.

As a habit to be studied.

They knew which officers resented winter assignments and drank more heavily because of it. They knew which nights patrols shortened when the wind made visibility impossible. They knew the rhythm of telegraph messages—morning reports, weekly inventories, occasional greetings between distant posts traveling along the wire.

They knew when riverboats arrived heavy with supplies.

They knew when ice made those arrivals impossible.

They knew the fort as routine.

After Bear Butte, the decision had not been shouted.

It had been spoken quietly in small circles where men considered the lessons of the winter.

The Army had learned how to destroy villages.

The Plains would learn how to interrupt the Army.

Fort Randall would be the test.

* * *

Mato arrived in early December under the guise of trade.

He rode a broad circle before approaching, observing from bluffs that overlooked the river valley. Snow lay shallow across the prairie, not yet deep enough to hinder movement. Smoke from the fort's chimneys rose straight in the brittle air.

He counted sentries.

He watched the stable yard.

He noted how long the western gate remained unattended during the change of watch.

The fort was not careless.

But it was comfortable.

Comfort creates blindness.

* * *

On December twenty-fourth, sleds arrived from upriver traders bearing crates marked as holiday exchange from Fort Thompson.

The markings were familiar.

Such exchanges were not unusual. Whiskey moved easily between posts during winter months, softening isolation that stretched too long across empty country.

The officers received the crates with visible relief.

By late afternoon discipline loosened.

Laughter carried across the yard. Boots struck planks less firmly. The smell of alcohol drifted through the brittle air. Sentries leaned deeper into their coats, faces reddened, movements slower.

Scouts watching from beyond rifle range reported what they had hoped to see.

Opportunity.

The original plan had been Christmas night.

But precision favors adjustment.

The decision shifted quietly.

Move before darkness settled fully, while warmth dulled reflexes.

* * *

The outer lookouts were taken first.

Not with volleys.

Not with spectacle.

Two men approached under cover of wind, speaking softly as if bearing a message. Rifles were removed before comprehension fully formed. Snow absorbed the sound of the brief struggle.

The stable yard followed.

Horses were secured quickly. Reins cut and replaced.

Without horses, pursuit dies before it begins.

Mato moved with the second wave, boots pressing carefully into snow already marked by routine tracks. Lamps flickered against the barrack walls. Voices rose unevenly inside.

Entry was controlled.

Doors opened before alarms spread. Resistance flared in brief pockets—a shouted warning cut short; a rifle discharged once into ceiling timber—then quieted again.

The cold swallowed sound beyond the walls.

The goal was not spectacle.

It was erasure.

Within a short span, the fort belonged to silence.

* * *

The telegraph room was entered intact.

Mato stepped inside behind two others. The wire hummed faintly in the winter air, carrying distant routine between posts that believed the continent orderly.

They did not smash the equipment.

They did not burn it.

Instead, lines were cut carefully—enough to sever immediate communication, not enough to advertise sabotage. Tools were replaced where they had rested. Snow brushed from the thresholds.

On the desk lay a prepared message written in a steady English hand.

It reported that the garrison had moved toward the Black Hills in response to unrest among miners. It noted expectation of replacement within the week.

Confusion is more powerful than chaos.

Mato rested his fingers lightly against the telegraph key before it was stilled. He did not understand the machinery completely.

But he understood what they were doing.

They were not defeating soldiers in open field.

They were interrupting narrative.

* * *

Bodies were moved before dawn.

Wagons loaded quietly. Horses harnessed and led away in staggered lines to avoid deep tracks. The frozen river carried sound poorly; wind erased what little remained.

The dead were taken to a remote bluff along the Missouri and concealed beneath drifting snow.

Not meant to vanish forever.

Meant to be discovered later—when discovery would fracture assumption.

Personal effects were burned in controlled pits. Weapons and ammunition redistributed. Supplies inventoried and divided with discipline.

Nothing was left to suggest battle.

* * *

When morning came, Fort Randall stood intact.

Doors closed.

Barracks orderly.

From a distance it appeared inactive—but not destroyed.

Snow softened every trace.

Several days passed before unease crept in.

Settlers waiting on river shipments approached cautiously. They found empty quarters. Drafted telegraph notes. No smoke from cook fires. No visible damage.

At first there was confusion.

Then suspicion.

Telegraph lines were repaired. Messages sent. Replies delayed.

By then riders were already moving—south and west and north.

The delay had done its work.

* * *

At Bear Butte, word arrived without ceremony.

Red Cloud listened without visible reaction.

"How long before they understand?" he asked.

Spotted Tail considered the distances involved.

"Long enough."

Messengers departed that same night.

To watchers near Fort Robinson.

To observers at Fort Laramie.

To Cheyenne bands along the Powder River.

To southern tribes waiting for proof.

And north—across the Medicine Line—to Sitting Bull.

Be ready.

* * *

Mato remained at Fort Randall through the first quiet days of occupation.

No banners flew above its walls.

No proclamations were made.

Smoke rose from chimneys again—controlled and deliberate. Patrol routes were adjusted. Sentries posted in patterns unfamiliar to any who had once manned the post.

He stood on the rampart at dusk and looked down at the Missouri sealed beneath ice.

He had grown up watching forts rise like scars across the land.

Now he watched one change allegiance without a battle echoing across the Plains.

This was different from Greasy Grass.

That had been decisive.

This was structural.

A regiment destroyed invites retaliation.

A fort quietly removed invites uncertainty.

If one post could vanish from Washington's certainty—

What would happen when others did?

Below him the river moved beneath its frozen surface, silent above and restless below.

So was the continent.

Chapter 14 - Fort Robinson

Fort Robinson sat colder than Randall.

Higher ground. Harsher wind. No broad river below to soften isolation. The post rose from stone and hard earth, its walls squared against weather that showed no mercy. Even in stillness it felt alert.

Which was precisely why Crazy Horse chose it.

After Bear Butte the sequence had been outlined quietly. Randall would test confusion. Robinson would test control.

Yet one uncertainty lingered. Fort Robinson did not behave like the others. Its command was disciplined. Its routines tighter. Intelligence gathered from scouts and traders was thinner than anyone preferred.

Debate began to circle.

Crazy Horse ended it before it hardened.

"I will go to them," he said.

Red Cloud answered immediately.

"You are too important."

"That is why."

Spotted Tail watched him closely.

"They will watch you."

"They will watch only me," Crazy Horse said. "And not what gathers elsewhere."

It was not surrender.

It was insertion.

* * *

He rode into Fort Robinson beneath a flag of negotiation before winter sealed the land.

The Army recorded it as progress. Newspapers in the East suggested the Plains were calming at last. Officers wrote careful reports noting the arrival of the famous Oglala leader and hinting that resistance might soon dissolve into cooperation.

Inside Lakota circles the meaning was different.

Crazy Horse had not come to surrender.

He had come to observe.

* * *

Valentine McGillycuddy met him in the yard.

The doctor had treated soldiers and tribesmen alike. He understood the Plains better than most officers stationed there, though he trusted few of its leaders completely.

"You understand your position?" he asked.

"Yes."

Confinement was deliberate but not cruel. Guards were careful. Sentries doubled after nightfall. Conversations were watched with polite suspicion.

Crazy Horse spoke little.

He watched everything.

Guard rotations.

The location of the armory.

Which soldiers complained most about the cold.

Where telegraph lines entered the command building.

The distance between the guardhouse and the outer gate.

McGillycuddy visited often.

"How do you feel?"

"Strong enough."

"Do you regret coming?"

"No."

The doctor believed he was tending a man contained.

He did not realize he was standing inside design.

* * *

Then word reached Robinson.

Fort Randall had fallen.

At first the news arrived wrapped in confusion—desertion, administrative failure, miscommunication. But confirmation followed quickly.

The post stood intact.

The garrison did not.

Security at Robinson tightened at once.

Patrols doubled.

Sentries walked their posts with colder discipline.

Officers spoke openly of transferring Crazy Horse eastward, where his influence could no longer reach the Plains.

The timeline shortened.

Extraction could not wait.

* * *

The night chosen for movement came bitter and wind-scoured. Snow drifted across the yard and blurred shapes along the outer wall.

Orders arrived to move Crazy Horse from the guardhouse.

Inside the building soldiers argued quietly over procedure. Some believed he should be restrained immediately. Others insisted the transfer remain orderly.

Crazy Horse refused to rise.

Not violently.

Simply refusing.

Hands grabbed his shoulders. A shove followed. A struggle flared in the narrow doorway.

Private William Gentles lunged forward.

The bayonet entered deep.

The sound was small.

Crazy Horse collapsed against the boards.

Blood spread dark beneath him.

For a moment the room froze.

McGillycuddy was summoned at once.

He knelt and examined the wound quickly.

Grave.

But not instantly fatal.

"He will not survive," the doctor told the nearest officer.

The statement passed through the room like final judgment.

Outside, the fort had already begun to fracture.

* * *

Warriors aligned with the Bear Butte council moved through the darkness as planned. Barrack doors burst open in sudden bursts of noise. Shots cracked across the yard, drawing soldiers outward into confusion.

Robinson did not fall in silence.

But the fighting was brief.

Snow muffled the gunfire. Officers attempted to form defensive lines and found their men already scattered across the compound.

By dawn the fort was secured.

Telegraph lines were under new control.

The flag was lowered.

* * *

Within a room removed from the yard, McGillycuddy worked through the night.

The wound was cleaned.

Packed.

Bound tightly.

Crazy Horse drifted between breath and darkness.

"You must live," the doctor murmured once, unsure whether he spoke to the man or to the consequence of his survival.

Outside the fort, soldiers who had escaped carried certainty with them.

Crazy Horse was dead.

Private Gentles swore it.

Officers repeated it.

Reports were drafted before doubt could take root.

McGillycuddy left days later under orders to confirm the death.

He did not contradict the account.

He carried it.

* * *

Across the Plains the story traveled quickly.

Crazy Horse had died resisting the Army.

Grief spread through the camps.

But something else moved with it.

The circles that had begun quietly after Bear Butte formed again.

Men and women gathered in widening rings beneath the winter sky. Songs passed between tribes that had once spoken only in wary trade. Movements repeated from camp to camp until the rhythm became shared.

Some traders struggled to describe what they saw.

"They dance for ghosts," one told a river merchant.

An Army scout wrote the phrase in his field notebook.

Ghost Dance.

The words were imperfect.

But they endured.

Within the camps the dance was not about ghosts.

It was about return.

Of buffalo.

Of balance.

Of ancestors walking without wounds.

* * *

Mato heard of Crazy Horse's death while riding along the Platte.

The news struck him like vertigo.

He rode hard toward Robinson, uncertain whether he approached farewell or truth.

Days later he crossed the outer perimeter and saw smoke rising from chimneys that no longer answered to Washington.

Inside a quiet room, Crazy Horse breathed slowly.

"You are not gone," Mato said.

"Not yet."

Relief brought no celebration.

Only weight.

The world believed him dead.

And the world would act on that belief.

Snow lay deep against the walls of Fort Robinson.

Riders were already moving toward Fort Laramie.

Southward, Comanche and Kiowa prepared.

Telegraph lines hesitated under unfamiliar hands.

The Ghost Dance spread faster than wire.

Fort Randall had shifted.

Fort Robinson had fallen.

And now something less visible—and more powerful—was moving across the Plains.

The Army had fought warriors before.

It had not yet faced a people aligning in spirit.

When Washington finally chose to stop the Ghost Dance, it would not be striking at ritual.

It would be striking at cohesion.

And that would change everything.

Chapter 15 - Washington

Winter arrived differently in Washington City.

Snow settled along broad avenues cut deliberately across the capital decades earlier. Government buildings rose from the landscape in pale stone, their columns stark against the gray sky. Carriages moved steadily between departments, wheels grinding through slush while clerks hurried beneath coats pulled tight against the cold.

Distance softened the Plains.

From Washington, the frontier rarely appeared as landscape.

It appeared as reports.

Columns of ink.

Lists of supplies.

Casualty numbers.

Requests for funding.

For years the war beyond the Missouri had been understood as a series of disturbances—local conflicts managed through the rotation of troops and occasional treaties.

After the summer of 1876, those assumptions began to weaken.

After the winter that followed, they began to collapse.

* * *

The first report that unsettled the War Department arrived quietly.

A telegraph from the Missouri frontier described irregular communication with Fort Randall. At first the explanation seemed simple enough—winter damage to telegraph lines, illness among the garrison, perhaps a delay in resupply.

Such disruptions were not unusual.

Yet a second message followed days later.

Then a third.

Each carried a similar detail.

No officer from Randall had confirmed the situation directly.

By early February the department ordered riders dispatched to determine the condition of the post.

The riders did not return quickly.

* * *

Other concerns began to accumulate.

Military dispatches from the northern Plains reported unusual movement among Lakota and Cheyenne bands. Patrols described villages that appeared briefly and vanished before engagement. Telegraph crews reported sections of line cut in ways that suggested intention rather than accident.

These were not the patterns of scattered raiding.

They suggested coordination.

Still, many officials resisted the implication.

Frontier reports were often exaggerated. The Plains were vast. Confusion was common.

But the next message forced reconsideration.

* * *

Communication from Fort Robinson arrived late and incomplete.

The report described the death of Crazy Horse during an attempted transfer from the guardhouse. The account was brief and written under visible strain. It confirmed the bayonet wound delivered by Private William Gentles and stated that the prisoner had died soon afterward.

Under ordinary circumstances such a report might have closed the matter.

Instead, it raised new questions.

Subsequent dispatches failed to describe the condition of the fort with clarity. Some messages referred to heightened security. Others mentioned irregular patrol conditions. A few simply stopped where telegraph transmission faltered.

Within the War Department, maps began appearing more frequently across conference tables.

Pins marked the positions of forts along the frontier.

Lines traced telegraph routes stretching westward from the Mississippi.

Supply depots were noted beside railheads advancing steadily across Kansas and Nebraska.

The system that supported the Army became visible there.

And the system appeared unsettled.

* * *

In one closed meeting, an officer who had served on the Plains spoke plainly.

"They are not fighting us the way they did before."

The statement drew quiet attention.

"What do you mean?" a civilian official asked.

"They are not concentrating their villages where we can strike them," the officer replied. "They are moving constantly. Watching our posts. Cutting communication lines. Disrupting supply."

He paused before adding the thought that troubled him most.

"They are studying us."

The phrase lingered longer than anyone expected.

For decades the Army had assumed the advantage of structure. Forts anchored the frontier. Telegraph wires carried orders faster than riders. Railroads moved troops with growing efficiency.

These systems had been built precisely because the Plains were vast.

If those systems were now being targeted deliberately, the advantage could narrow quickly.

* * *

New reports deepened the unease.

Scouts described gatherings of tribes that had rarely cooperated in earlier years. Lakota, Cheyenne, Arapaho, and southern observers were said to be meeting in larger circles than before.

At first the gatherings appeared religious.

Dancing.

Singing.

Night assemblies repeated across camps separated by hundreds of miles.

One field officer wrote the description in a tone meant to diminish its importance.

"Native enthusiasm centered on a so-called Ghost Dance."

The term appeared again in later reports.

No one in Washington fully understood it.

But several details were noted carefully.

The gatherings were spreading.

They crossed tribal divisions.

And they appeared to strengthen unity rather than weaken it.

* * *

By early spring the situation could no longer be dismissed as scattered unrest.

The unexplained silence from Fort Randall, the uncertain conditions reported at Fort Robinson, and repeated disruptions along telegraph routes formed a pattern too consistent to ignore.

A senior official summarized the concern in a memorandum circulated quietly among department heads:

If these events represent intentional coordination among the Plains tribes, the matter must be regarded not as regional disturbance but as organized resistance.

The phrase carried weight.

Organized resistance suggested something larger than rebellion.

It suggested strategy.

* * *

President Ulysses S. Grant read the memorandum without visible reaction.

Ulysses S. Grant understood war better than most men in Washington. During the American Civil War, he had seen how systems—railroads, telegraph networks, supply depots—shaped campaigns more than individual battles.

If those systems were now being disrupted deliberately across the Plains, the problem would not be solved by a single expedition.

It would require something larger.

And larger responses carried consequences.

The nation had only recently emerged from one continental war.

Few in Congress were eager to imagine another conflict stretching across half the continent.

* * *

That evening the President stood near the window of the Executive Mansion and looked westward across the darkened city.

Somewhere beyond the Mississippi—beyond the long grass and frozen rivers—men he had never met were testing the limits of a nation that believed itself inevitable.

For years Washington had treated the Plains as a question already answered.

Now the question was returning.

Not with a single battle.

But with uncertainty.

And uncertainty, Grant knew, could spread faster than cavalry.

* * *

Far from Washington, along the Missouri where Mato had once watched the forts rise, the river continued its slow passage toward the south.

Telegraph wires hummed quietly above the frozen ground.

Riders moved between camps that had begun to think together rather than apart.

And across the Plains, the circles of the Ghost Dance widened beneath the winter stars.

The Army had fought warriors before.

It had not yet faced a people learning to move as one.

Chapter 16 - The Government Responds

Spring moved slowly across the Plains that year.

Snow withdrew unevenly from the valleys. Grass appeared first along the south-facing ridges, pale and flattened from winter. Rivers broke their ice with dull reports that echoed across miles of empty country. What had seemed frozen and immovable through the long cold months began to move again.

The Army moved with it.

Orders traveled west from Washington in deliberate language that concealed their urgency. Supply trains expanded along railheads in Nebraska and Kansas. New shipments of ammunition moved toward frontier depots. Telegraph operators were instructed to report interruptions immediately—not in routine summaries, but in direct messages to departmental headquarters.

The frontier, once managed in scattered districts, was now treated as a single theater.

For several years the government had assumed that defeating a few hostile bands would restore stability to the Plains.

Now the problem appeared different.

Reports no longer described isolated villages or scattered raids.

They described patterns.

* * *

The unexplained silence from Fort Randall remained unresolved.

Riders sent to investigate had not returned within the expected time. Telegraph crews working along the Missouri reported lines cut in several places where winter storms had caused no damage.

At Fort Robinson, communication arrived in fragments. Officers confirmed the death of Crazy Horse but offered little clarity about the condition of the post itself. Patrol reports contradicted one another. Some suggested heightened security. Others described activity that did not match official explanations.

The Army had faced uncertainty before.

But uncertainty rarely spread across such distance at once.

* * *

Maps appeared constantly now on the tables of the War Department.

The frontier was marked in a lattice of thin lines and careful symbols. Forts stood at intervals along the Missouri and across the Platte country. Telegraph wires traced long connections between them. Railroads extended westward in dark strokes representing steel laid across prairie.

For years the strength of the United States had rested on that system.

Forts secured territory.

Telegraphs carried command.

Railroads moved men and supplies.

Together they formed the structure that allowed a nation to govern land it could not yet see completely.

Now that structure appeared to tremble.

Not broken.

But tested.

***

Field officers began using language that unsettled their superiors.

One dispatch described tribal movements that "suggest observation of our positions rather than simple evasion."

Another reported telegraph lines cut in places where repair would be delayed longest.

A third officer wrote bluntly that the tribes seemed to be "attacking the system itself rather than individual garrisons."

Such phrasing was rarely welcome in official correspondence.

It implied that the enemy understood the machinery of the nation.

***

The War Department responded with greater concentration of force.

Additional regiments were ordered west from posts once considered distant from the Plains conflict. Rail transport expanded to move infantry quickly toward Nebraska and Dakota Territory. Civilian contractors were hired to repair telegraph lines with greater speed and to guard them while they worked.

At the same time, Indian agents across the reservation system received new instructions.

Gatherings were to be monitored carefully.

Travel between bands discouraged.

Reports concerning the so-called Ghost Dance were to be forwarded immediately to territorial authorities.

At first these instructions seemed excessive.

But the reports continued.

***

The Ghost Dance appeared in dispatches with increasing frequency.

At first it was described as religious excitement—a ritual revival that occasionally spread among tribes during hardship.

But new reports contained details that troubled officials reading them.

The gatherings were not confined to one tribe.

Lakota, Cheyenne, and Arapaho attended the same ceremonies. Observers reported that songs and movements were repeated across camps separated by hundreds of miles.

Even more unsettling was the tone of the participants.

Morale among the tribes appeared to be strengthening.

The dance was not weakening resistance.

It was binding it.

* * *

One memorandum circulated quietly among senior officers summarized the concern in language more direct than usual:

If present developments continue, the tribes of the Plains may soon possess both the spiritual cohesion and operational mobility necessary to sustain prolonged resistance.

The phrase spiritual cohesion appeared more than once in the document.

It was an unfamiliar concern for military planners accustomed to measuring strength in numbers and rifles.

Yet the evidence was difficult to dismiss.

Where the Ghost Dance appeared, tribal cooperation seemed to follow.

Where cooperation grew, the Army encountered greater difficulty predicting movement.

* * *

President Ulysses S. Grant listened to these reports with measured patience.

During the American Civil War, he had learned that destroying infrastructure—railroads, supply depots, communication lines—could cripple forces larger than one's own.

The possibility that such methods might now be used against the United States did not escape him.

But the nation had grown confident in its expansion.

Few in Congress believed the Plains tribes capable of such coordination.

Grant was less certain.

* * *

While Washington debated, events beyond the frontier continued to unfold.

Traders moving north from the Platte reported that the Ghost Dance had reached camps along the Powder River.

Scouts along the Yellowstone described riders traveling between tribes that had seldom cooperated in earlier years.

Telegraph crews repairing damaged lines claimed they had seen signals along distant ridges—fires appearing and vanishing with unusual regularity.

Each report alone might have been dismissed.

Together they suggested something forming beyond Washington's understanding.

* * *

Late in the spring a new dispatch arrived from the northern frontier.

It had first been carried by rider, then transmitted along a telegraph line recently repaired near the Canadian border.

The message was brief.

Its meaning was not.

It reported that a group of Hunkpapa Lakota had crossed southward from beyond the Medicine Line.

Among them, according to the scout who observed the movement, rode a man believed long removed from the conflict.

The name appeared near the end of the report.

Sitting Bull.

For several years he had remained beyond American reach in the territories north of the border, watching events from a distance that allowed patience.

Now he was said to be returning.

The report did not describe his purpose.

But those who read it understood the implication.

If the tribes of the Plains were already gathering in spirit, the return of Sitting Bull could transform that spirit into direction.

* * *

That evening the telegraph carried the message west and east in equal measure.

Across the Plains, riders moved through grass newly rising from the thaw.

Circles formed again beneath the darkening sky.

Songs passed between camps.

And somewhere along the northern horizon, a man long believed distant began riding toward a land no longer the same as when he had left it.

The government had begun to respond.

But the Plains were already moving.

Chapter 17 - The Return

Word reached Canada in fragments.

Fort Randall taken.

Fort Robinson fallen.

Crazy Horse dead — so the soldiers claimed.

Sitting Bull listened without visible reaction.

Snow pressed hard against the edges of camp. Smoke from low fires drifted flat through the bitter northern air. The Hunkpapa had endured the winter deliberately, neither hiding nor provoking, watching from beyond the Medicine Line as the United States steadied itself after the shock of Greasy Grass.

Now the reports suggested something else.

Washington was not steady.

Forts along the Missouri corridor had fallen into silence. Telegraph lines faltered. Riders arriving from the south spoke of night gatherings spreading across the Plains—circles of singing and movement the soldiers had begun calling the Ghost Dance.

At first the phrase had been used lightly.

Almost dismissively.

Now it appeared in formal dispatches.

Intertribal assemblies.

Spiritual agitation.

Possible coordination beneath religious cover.

Officers who had laughed at the phrase weeks earlier were no longer laughing.

Sitting Bull rose from the fire without ceremony.

He had watched long enough.

He turned south.

* * *

The Hunkpapa did not move like fugitives.

They traveled as a people accustomed to distance—steady, deliberate, aware of the country beneath their horses. They followed the broad curve of the Missouri without announcing intention, yet without concealment.

They did not ride in war formation.

They rode as if returning home.

Along the river settlements watched their passage with unease. Traders counted horses from a distance. Ranchers spoke quietly of the movement to nearby agencies. Telegraph operators passed brief messages eastward along the wire.

The name in those messages traveled faster than the riders themselves.

Sitting Bull was returning.

* * *

The Standing Rock Reservation lay directly along his path.

Indian agents Bull Head and Red Tomahawk had been under increasing pressure from Washington to assert visible authority. Reports of Ghost Dance gatherings had multiplied. Ranchers complained of cattle taken or driven off. Military officers warned that spiritual unity among the tribes might harden into armed resistance without warning.

The agency already felt brittle when Sitting Bull arrived.

The agents decided to act quickly.

The arrest was meant to be contained.

Symbolic.

A demonstration of federal authority before winter fully released the land.

It unraveled immediately.

Voices rose within the small cluster of agency buildings. Lakota followers moved instinctively toward Sitting Bull. Hands shifted toward weapons not yet drawn.

A shot cracked.

Later no one agreed who fired first.

Gunfire spread in confusion. Snow kicked up around boots and hooves. Seven of Sitting Bull's followers fell within moments. Bull Head staggered backward, mortally wounded. Red Tomahawk forced his way through the chaos.

Sitting Bull was struck.

He fell hard into the snow.

Blood spread quickly across the white ground.

He did not rage.

He did not plead.

With the last clarity that remained, he summoned Big Foot.

"Continue south," he said. "Do not stop."

Leadership passed in urgency, not ceremony.

By the time the firing ceased, Sitting Bull was dead.

* * *

But the movement did not falter.

It sharpened.

Big Foot understood two truths at once.

The plan remained.

The danger had multiplied.

The 7th Cavalry Regiment, rebuilt and reinforced after the disaster at Greasy Grass, now moved along the river corridor with vengeance threaded through its purpose. Officers spoke openly of suppressing not only armed resistance but the Ghost Dance itself.

One officer at Fort Yates wrote bluntly in his field report:

The so-called Ghost Dance unites tribes previously divided.

This cannot be permitted to continue unchecked.

The dance had moved from curiosity to threat.

* * *

Big Foot angled southwest toward the Pine Ridge Reservation, where Red Cloud had already agreed that consolidation would follow if pressure mounted.

Snow began falling heavily enough to blur tracks.

Scouts rode ahead and returned uncertain.

"We lost them," one admitted.

Big Foot's unease deepened.

He sent his fastest rider ahead.

A young messenger known among the camps as Little Buffalo.

The boy rode through wind and drifting snow as if distance had ceased to exist.

* * *

Little Buffalo reached Pine Ridge before dawn.

His horse trembled from exhaustion. His voice did not.

Red Cloud listened as the rider spoke of Sitting Bull's death and the movement of the Seventh Cavalry.

There was no outward display of grief.

Red Cloud stood.

Orders followed immediately.

Warriors mounted before the boy had finished speaking.

Grief would come later.

Movement came first.

* * *

The Seventh Cavalry anticipated Big Foot's route and intercepted near Wounded Knee Creek.

Snow lay thick across the valley. Wind cut sideways across the frozen ground, reducing distance to shifting shadows.

But this was not a band surprised and disarmed.

Big Foot had been warned.

Warriors positioned themselves ahead of the main body. Rifles remained close at hand. The camp did not surrender its weapons.

The standoff tightened.

An officer demanded disarmament.

Lakota leaders answered cautiously.

A shot rang out.

Again, no one later agreed who fired first.

* * *

The Seventh deployed its Hotchkiss gun along the ridge.

The first shell tore into snow and earth with violence unfamiliar even to seasoned warriors.

The second exploded closer.

But the cavalry had misjudged one thing.

Red Cloud's riders arrived sooner than expected.

They rose through drifts and shallow draws along the flank, pressing up the ridge with relentless momentum. The artillery crews did not anticipate attack from that direction.

Horses screamed.

Gunners pivoted too late.

Close fighting swallowed the ridge.

One Hotchkiss gun swung wildly before being seized. Another discharged prematurely, the shell bursting among cavalry ranks when its aim faltered.

Smoke and snow collapsed together into gray violence.

The Seventh Cavalry fractured.

* * *

When the firing finally ceased, bodies lay across the frozen valley on both sides.

But the Hotchkiss guns stood silent in Lakota hands.

In the confusion, Big Foot disappeared.

Two days later, after the blizzard relented, scouts found him frozen upright against a drift, rifle still clutched in his hands.

He had never surrendered the fight.

He was given scaffold burial.

The soldiers were left where they had fallen.

The choice was deliberate.

Discovery would speak louder than explanation.

* * *

At Pine Ridge, Red Cloud absorbed the survivors without ceremony.

Women.

Children.

Warriors.

Grief pressed heavily through the camps.

But design did not pause.

Sitting Bull was dead.

Big Foot was dead.

Crazy Horse was believed dead.

Washington would assume the leadership shattered.

Instead, consolidation deepened.

The north had guarded.

The center had seized.

Now blood sealed commitment.

* * *

The Ghost Dance circles grew larger after Wounded Knee.

Not because people believed shirts made them invulnerable.

But because they needed to feel each other breathing in rhythm.

The Army's attempts to suppress the gatherings only confirmed their power. Each arrest, each warning order, each accusation of insurrection drew more people into the circles.

The dance was no longer renewal alone.

It had become quiet defiance.

Across the Plains the term now appeared openly in military reports.

Ghost Dance.

Capitalized.

Linked to unrest.

Linked to campaign.

* * *

When word of the battle at Wounded Knee reached Washington, the reaction was immediate and fractured.

Telegraph reports conflicted. Casualty counts shifted. Some dispatches described massacre. Others insisted it had been a pitched engagement.

But one fact settled quickly.

The Seventh Cavalry had been broken again.

Not in isolation.

Within sequence.

* * *

President Ulysses S. Grant stared down at the map spread across the War Department table.

The Medicine Line had not contained the crisis.

It had merely repositioned it.

This was no longer a frontier disturbance.

The Plains were not reacting.

They were advancing.

Chapter 18 - The Plains Open

Winter did not release the field at Wounded Knee Creek quickly.

Snow drifted over cavalry blue and Lakota hide alike, softening shape but not memory. The ridge where the Hotchkiss gun had stood remained scarred dark against the white, as if the earth itself had absorbed the violence and refused to smooth it away.

Red Cloud climbed that ridge before leaving.

He did not linger.

"The ridge is ours," he said quietly.

Then he looked out across the valley—over the frozen creek, over the scattered lodges below—and added,

"Now the Plains must be."

Riders departed before the blizzard fully cleared.

* * *

At Pine Ridge Reservation, consolidation began without proclamation.

Big Foot's survivors were absorbed as if they had always belonged there. Women were placed in lodges without ceremony. Children were wrapped in blankets and fed before questions were asked. The wounded were tended in silence. Rifles were counted. Ammunition redistributed.

The captured Hotchkiss guns stood apart, half buried in drifted snow.

Men who had watched their shells tear through earth now examined them carefully.

Not with awe.

With study.

They disassembled what they could. They traced the weight of iron and the rhythm of loading. They measured distance with their eyes.

They understood something simple.

Power did not belong to whoever forged a weapon.

It belonged to whoever learned its use.

* * *

Messengers rode south and west before the valley finished freezing.

The signal was no longer subtle. - Move.

* * *

Fort Laramie heard before it understood.

Telegraph wires carried fragments.

Seventh broken again.

Casualties uncertain.

Lakota mobilizing.

Supply trains from the east failed to arrive on schedule. Patrols sent westward did not return. Woodcutting parties found their paths blocked by mounted riders who did not engage, only observed.

Water access outside the walls became contested ground.

Red Cloud did not waste men on spectacle.

He strangled the fort first.

* * *

Mato rode along the Platte River in late winter, feeling the cold bite through his gloves as he studied the fort from a distance.

He watched which doors opened at dawn.

Which officers rode out to inspect pickets.

Which wagons were turned away by uncertainty.

The telegraph still functioned.

But its messages grew shorter.

More urgent.

By the time engagement began in earnest, the garrison was already cut off from confidence.

Ammunition was rationed.

Reinforcements were requested twice.

No answer came that satisfied.

When resistance finally fractured, it did so quickly.

The flag came down without ceremony.

The fort was not burned.

It was taken.

* * *

Inside, Mato walked past orderly barracks and stacked crates.

He felt not triumph.

He felt recalibration.

Each fort that shifted changed the geometry of the Plains.

With Laramie fallen, Fort Fetterman stood exposed.

* * *

The Cheyenne and Arapaho arrived first.

Lakota riders followed close behind.

They did not rush the fort.

Instead, they placed the captured Hotchkiss guns within sight of the perimeter.

They did not fire.

They simply let the garrison see them.

We can use what you use.

Inside the fort, morale thinned faster than supplies.

Officers debated holding position or attempting withdrawal. Some argued reinforcements would arrive. Others admitted privately that no column could reach them in time without leaving another region bare.

When the first shell was fired—not into the fort, but just beyond its outer works—the concussion shook confidence more than earth.

The garrison abandoned the post under cover of darkness.

By dawn, another fort stood silent.

* * *

The shock traveled south faster than thaw.

Quanah Parker listened to reports of Laramie and Fetterman with the stillness of someone who had waited through too many winters.

The north had not flared and collapsed.

It had expanded.

Kiowa leaders gathered.

Comanche war captains conferred.

Kiowa-Apache allies moved quietly along familiar trails.

No proclamation announced the change.

Movement itself announced it.

* * *

Fort Sill tightened its defenses.

Fort Supply lost reliable contact with its outposts.

Fort Griffin watched cattle trails thin as ranchers began pushing herds south in uneasy anticipation.

Fort Dodge reported desertions before engagement even began.

Not every fort fell in battle.

Some fell because their garrisons calculated the odds.

Fear can accomplish what artillery cannot.

* * *

Across Texas, ranchers muttered that the frontier felt unmoored.

Cattle drives slowed.

Freight wagons doubled their guards.

Rail shipments hesitated at junctions in Kansas and Nebraska.

The weather was not the only thing freezing.

Credit began to freeze as well.

* * *

By March the pattern in Washington could no longer be dismissed.

Fort Randall.

Fort Robinson.

Wounded Knee.

Fort Laramie.

Fort Fetterman.

Southern posts destabilizing.

Railroad executives arrived in person, no longer satisfied with telegrams. They spoke of halted expansion, of insurance rates doubling, of investors losing confidence in western lines.

Cattle barons threatened private militias if federal response lagged.

Southern politicians warned that stripping troops from Reconstruction states could reopen wounds barely scarred.

President Ulysses S. Grant faced arithmetic he did not like.

The Army could not respond everywhere at once.

The nation could not afford paralysis.

And yet paralysis crept in.

* * *

At Fort Randall, now under tribal control, Mato stood over maps spread across a rough-hewn table.

He had watched forts rise across the Plains when he was a boy.

Now he watched them connect differently.

Leaders no longer spoke of raids.

They spoke of corridors.

The Missouri River secured.

The Black Hills held.

The Powder River corridor open.

Southern Indian Territory destabilized in alignment.

For the first time, Mato heard discussion of boundaries not as confinement.

But as recognition.

Not where we must stay.

Where they must acknowledge.

No one said the word nation aloud.

But it moved between sentences like smoke.

* * *

Rail crews west of North Platte refused to lay track without military escort.

Telegraph wires were cut in short, deliberate segments—never long enough to suggest chaos beyond repair, but frequent enough to create hesitation.

Trains slowed.

Insurance rates rose.

Merchants in Missouri began limiting credit extended into Kansas.

In eastern newspapers the language shifted.

At first: uprising.

Then: rebellion.

Then, increasingly:

Who governs the Plains?

* * *

That question unsettled Washington more deeply than any artillery shell.

Congress convened in emergency session.

Some demanded total war.

Sweep the territory.

Reassert dominion at any cost.

Others warned of bankruptcy, of political fracture, of Southern instability if troops were stripped away from Reconstruction.

Rail interests demanded decisive action.

Reconstruction advocates urged caution.

Grant refused to use the word surrender.

But one evening, in a closed room with maps spread across a long table, he asked quietly:

"What are they asking for?"

No one answered.

Because the answer had not yet been spoken.

* * *

By early May the last major southern post under coordinated pressure shifted.

Not always in battle.

Often through calculation.

Often through fear.

Fort flags came down across the center of the continent.

In Washington, maps were redrawn in pencil.

On the Plains, riders moved without paper.

* * *

The first true thaw began.

Ice cracked in long seams.

Water moved beneath it, slow but undeniable.

They had taken territory.

Now came the harder question.

Could they hold it?

Chapter 19 - The Terms

Washington had asked a question, but the answer did not come from Washington. It formed on the Plains.

The thaw along the Platte came slowly that spring. Snow lingered in shaded cuts while the open ground turned to mud beneath horse hooves. The wind still carried winter in it, though the sun now held longer in the sky.

At Fort Laramie the walls stood unchanged. The flag above the parade ground no longer belonged to the United States, but the buildings remained. The telegraph still functioned. Traders still passed through. And the old command office still held the long table where Army officers had once debated removal policy.

Now the table held maps.

Red Cloud stood beside it, tracing the Missouri River with one finger. Across from him stood Quanah Parker, recently arrived from the southern Plains after a long ride north. Spotted Tail listened quietly. Others stood around them—Cheyenne, Kiowa, Arapaho. They had fought separately for years. Now they spoke together.

The war had delivered something none of them had expected: territory. But territory alone was not enough. It had to be defined. It had to be defended. And now, unexpectedly, it had to be explained.

Near the wall stood Mato Ska with paper and ink. He had begun keeping record in both ways—charcoal on hide and English script on paper. Crazy Horse had told him simply, "You write."

Red Cloud spoke first. "We do not want their towns."

He pointed again to the Missouri.

"Their river towns may remain."

Quanah nodded slowly. "We want the land."

"The buffalo," someone added.

"And no forts."

Spotted Tail looked toward the telegraph office visible through the window. "They will ask for the rail."

Quanah gave a short laugh. "They always do."

Crazy Horse stood apart from the table, quiet as he listened. The scar beneath his ribs pulled when he breathed too deeply, though he did not show it. At last, he spoke.

"They can run their rail," he said, "so long as they ask."

Mato wrote the words down.

Rail allowed by agreement. Not by right.

The room grew quiet again. Red Cloud looked toward Mato.

"Write the rivers."

Mato dipped the pen again.

Missouri. Platte. Powder. Arkansas.

Natural boundaries. Not lines drawn by strangers.

When the writing was finished, Red Cloud folded the pages carefully.

"This will go east," he said.

There was only one man who could carry it.

Dr. Valentine McGillycuddy had arrived at Fort Laramie weeks earlier under escort after leaving Fort Robinson. He had expected imprisonment. Instead, he had been allowed to remain. The Plains leaders understood something Washington had not yet accepted: McGillycuddy moved between worlds. That made him useful.

Mato carried the folded pages to the small office near the parade ground where the doctor now worked. McGillycuddy looked up as he entered.

"You have something for me."

It was not a question.

Mato placed the packet on the desk. "You will take this to Washington."

McGillycuddy hesitated. "Do they know what this is?"

"No."

The doctor studied the young man for a long moment. "They will not like it."

"They do not have to like it."

McGillycuddy gave a faint, tired smile. "No," he said. "They only have to understand it."

He folded the pages again and placed them inside his coat.

Outside, the telegraph wire hummed softly in the wind.

* * *

Dr. Valentine McGillycuddy did not leave Fort Laramie quickly. He waited two days, not for permission but for weather.

Spring on the Plains came unevenly. Snow melted along the Platte valley while the higher ground remained locked in crusted drifts. Wagons stalled easily. Horses broke through soft ground where frost had only begun to release its grip.

The packet inside his coat felt heavier than its paper weight suggested. It was not merely a message. It was a boundary.

When he finally departed, he did so with a small escort arranged by the Plains leaders themselves. Lakota riders accompanied him east along the Platte corridor until the railhead was reached near Cheyenne. They rode in silence most of the way. The land was changing. Burned grass from winter fires stretched along the horizon. Meltwater cut shallow channels through frozen earth. Herds of antelope moved cautiously across the plains as if uncertain the long violence had truly passed.

On the second day they crossed the churned ground of a recent cavalry patrol—boot impressions, wagon ruts, and the wide arc of artillery wheels. The escort did not avoid it. They rode around it and let the tracks remain.

By the time they reached the rail line, the riders halted without ceremony. One of them nodded toward the train platform.

"Your road now."

McGillycuddy inclined his head in return. He did not ask their names. They did not offer them.

The train arrived in a plume of steam and iron noise that felt almost unnatural after weeks of prairie wind. The doctor boarded alone. The Plains fell away slowly behind him.

Across Nebraska and into Iowa the country thickened. Fences multiplied. Farmhouses appeared along the horizon. Telegraph poles marched beside the rail in disciplined lines. At every stop boys ran along the platform shouting headlines before the train had fully halted.

PLAINS IN REVOLT.

SEVENTH CAVALRY BROKEN AGAIN.

CONFEDERATE HAND SUSPECTED.

The rumors grew stranger the farther east he traveled.

CRAZY HORSE DEAD.

CRAZY HORSE ALIVE.

GHOST DANCE ARMIES.

INVULNERABLE SHIRTS.

McGillycuddy read none of the papers offered to him. He already knew the truth behind the rumors. It was not superstition that frightened Washington. It was organization.

The Plains leaders had not written a declaration of war.

They had written a proposal.

Chicago rose around the train two days later in smoke and steel. Beyond it the country thickened further—cities, factories, river traffic, the steady mechanical pulse of a nation that had nearly forgotten how wide the continent truly was.

By the time he reached Washington, the rumors had outrun him.

He was taken first to the War Department. The long table there was buried beneath maps. Red circles marked forts no longer flying federal colors. Black strokes marked broken rail corridors. Blue pins clung stubbornly to remaining garrisons like islands in a shrinking sea.

At the head of the table stood Ulysses S. Grant.

Grant looked up as the doctor entered. "You have come a long way."

McGillycuddy removed the folded packet from his coat. "So have they."

Grant gestured toward the table. "What are they asking for?"

The same question that had hung unanswered since the meeting weeks earlier now rested quietly in the room.

McGillycuddy unfolded the pages and read slowly: recognition of territorial sovereignty across defined Plains boundaries, control of the Missouri River within those boundaries, protection of buffalo herds, restriction—not elimination—of rail corridors, removal of federal forts, and recognition of tribal governance.

When he finished, the room did not erupt.

It cooled.

The Secretary of War spoke first. "You cannot recognize that."

Grant did not raise his voice. "Compared to what?"

The room understood the question. Compared to a continental war. Compared to destabilizing Reconstruction in the South. Compared to rail collapse across the center of the nation.

Grant studied the map again.

Dakotas. Wyoming. Nebraska. Kansas. Indian Territory. The Texas Panhandle.

A continental spine.

The Plains had not simply resisted. They had reorganized.

Grant looked again at McGillycuddy. "Will they negotiate?"

The doctor answered carefully. "They already are."

Grant nodded once. "Then we will reply."

For the first time since the end of the Civil War, the United States prepared to negotiate not from victory, but from calculation.

Outside the War Department, the telegraph wires hummed across the city. Soon they would carry a message west—not an order, but a response.

And somewhere beyond the Missouri, on land that Washington had once believed entirely its own, men waited to see what the United States would say next.

Chapter 20 - The Rumor

The room had not yet emptied when the intelligence officer spoke again.

"Mr. President… there is another matter."

Ulysses S. Grant did not immediately look up from the map spread across the table.

"There are always other matters."

The officer hesitated.

"It concerns Crazy Horse."

That name still carried weight in Washington.

Grant lifted his eyes. "Go on."

The officer placed two dispatches on the table.

"They disagree."

Grant glanced at them. "About what?"

"Whether he is dead."

The room grew still.

"The Army reports he died at Fort Robinson," the officer continued. "Bayonet wound. Witnessed by soldiers."

Grant nodded slightly. "That was my understanding."

"Yes, sir."

The officer tapped the second dispatch.

"But traders and scouts report sightings."

Grant read quickly. Riders claiming they had seen Crazy Horse among Lakota camps. Reports from agents who could not confirm the sightings—but could not dismiss them.

Grant set the paper down slowly.

"And which do you believe?"

"The Army believes him dead," the officer said carefully. Then he added, "But the Plains do not."

Grant leaned back in his chair.

"And what do you believe, Doctor?"

All eyes turned toward Valentine McGillycuddy.

The doctor had remained near the end of the table since reading the Plains demands. For a moment he did not answer.

"I treated the wound," he said at last.

The room leaned slightly toward him.

"It was severe. A bayonet beneath the ribs. Substantial blood loss."

"Fatal?" someone asked.

McGillycuddy considered the word.

"It should have been."

Grant watched him closely.

"But?"

The doctor met his gaze.

"But I have learned that the Plains do not measure survival the way we do."

Silence lingered.

Grant studied him. "So, you are not certain."

"No, sir."

Another officer slid a field report across the table.

"There are increasing reports of gatherings," he said.

Grant glanced at the page.

"Ghost Dance."

"Yes, sir."

"Religious excitement?"

"Perhaps." The officer hesitated. "Or something more organized."

Grant leaned back again.

"I do not believe in ghosts."

"No, sir."

"But my Army does."

The room absorbed that quietly. Fear, Grant knew, traveled through armies faster than orders.

He looked once more at McGillycuddy.

"If the man is alive," Grant said calmly, "then he remains the most important figure on the Plains."

No one disagreed.

Grant returned his attention to the map.

"Find out."

* * *

The telegraph carried uncertainty faster than certainty.

Within two days of Grant's instruction, messages began arriving from the western wires—short, incomplete, and often contradictory. At the War Department clerks pinned them to the same map already crowded with red circles and black slashes.

One dispatch from Fort Leavenworth reported increased movement among Lakota bands along the Platte.

Another from Fort Sidney mentioned gatherings near the old trading routes.

A trader's message forwarded from Cheyenne contained a single line that drew more attention than the others.

Crazy Horse seen near Laramie.

The message was unsigned. The War Department filed it anyway.

Rumors had filled the wires before. Most dissolved when examined closely. But more reports followed.

A rail agent in Nebraska heard the same claim from freight drivers moving west. A courier arriving in Omaha repeated it again.

Crazy Horse rides again.

By the end of the week the phrase had begun appearing in newspaper offices as well. Some editors printed it cautiously. Others treated it as spectacle.

THE DEAD WAR CHIEF RETURNS.

CRAZY HORSE RIDES AGAIN.

Most of the stories contradicted one another. Some claimed he led a Ghost Dance army. Others insisted the sighting was nothing more than drunken frontier gossip.

But the reports refused to disappear.

They multiplied.

In Washington, Grant read them without comment. Newspapers did not trouble him.

Field reports did.

Two scouts working for the Army's Department of the Platte submitted identical observations three days apart.

Large intertribal movement near Fort Laramie.

No hostile action reported.

No attempt to conceal numbers.

Grant read the reports twice.

If the Plains leaders were gathering openly at Laramie, it was not for war. Warriors preparing for battle did not concentrate themselves in a single visible place. They spread. They hid. They waited.

Grant looked again at the map.

Laramie stood at a hinge in the continent.

Rail.

Telegraph.

The Platte corridor.

If the Plains intended to send a message, that was where they would send it.

Across the city in the Executive Mansion, Grant finally spoke the thought aloud.

"If he is alive," he said quietly, "they will show him."

The Secretary of War frowned.

"You believe the rumors?"

"I believe the Plains understand theater," Grant replied.

He tapped the map once with his finger.

"If Crazy Horse lives, they will not hide him."

* * *

Outside Washington the telegraph wires stretched westward across the plains and mountains, carrying fragments of rumor faster than riders ever could.

But on the Plains, themselves, no telegraph carried the truth.

Riders carried it.

Along the Platte valley word moved from camp to camp. Leaders were gathering—Lakota, Cheyenne, Arapaho, and southern envoys from Comanche and Kiowa country. They came not as war parties, but to witness.

At Fort Laramie the parade ground stood quiet beneath the pale sky of early spring. The walls had not changed. The buildings had not changed.

Only the authority inside them had.

Messengers rode through the guard posts without challenge. Traders moved cautiously along the outer yards. Across the open ground men spoke quietly of the same question now unsettling Washington.

Was he alive?

Some said the soldiers had buried him.

Some said the soldiers had lied.

Others said the spirits had returned him.

Few claimed to know the truth.

They only knew that riders had been sent south.

And when those riders returned, they would not come alone.

Across the Plains the rumor continued to grow—not shouted, not proclaimed, but passed quietly from fire to fire.

Crazy Horse rides.

And when the man finally appeared, the rumor would not end.

It would become proof.

Chapter 21 - The Man Who Returned

Spring wind moved easily through Fort Laramie.

The fort had never been built to stop the wind. Its long barracks and low officer buildings formed a rough rectangle around the open parade ground, but the road that crossed it remained open to the plains beyond. Wagons passed through freely. Riders entered without ceremony.

Frontier forts were not castles.

They were crossroads.

That morning the wind carried dust from the Platte and the faint metallic hum of the telegraph wire stretching east toward the rail line.

Mato Ska stood inside the telegraph room with the operator. The man had finally allowed him to touch the key.

"Gently," the operator said.

Mato pressed the lever.

Click.

Pause.

Click-click.

The sound seemed too small to matter. Yet the operator nodded toward the wire.

"That noise will reach Omaha before sunset."

Mato imagined the signal racing across hundreds of miles of poles and wire—sound becoming language, language becoming history.

"I am slow," Mato said.

"Everyone is slow at first."

Outside, voices rose in the yard.

Not alarm.

Movement.

Mato stepped outside.

Riders had begun gathering along the open road that crossed the parade ground. Lakota and Cheyenne stood beside traders, scouts, and a handful of soldiers who had remained at the fort after its authority shifted. No one spoke loudly. They simply watched the southern horizon.

Word had traveled quietly for two days.

He is coming.

Some believed it. Some did not. But no one had left.

Near the old command building, Red Cloud stood beside Quanah Parker and Spotted Tail. They did not speak. They waited.

The rider appeared as a dark shape against the pale grasslands.

One horse.

No escort.

The distance closed slowly.

Mato felt the strange quiet spread across the parade ground. Even the traders seemed to understand that something larger than curiosity was unfolding.

The rider did not hurry. He crossed the open ground the way a man rides into a place he already knows.

Dust settled behind the horse's hooves.

As he came closer the scar beneath his ribs pulled with each breath, though no one could see it.

Crazy Horse rode into Fort Laramie without announcement.

No banner marked his arrival. No proclamation followed. He simply rode across the open parade ground and stopped beside the leaders waiting for him.

For a moment no one spoke.

Many of the men gathered there had believed him dead. Some still did.

The bayonet wound beneath his ribs had nearly ended him at Fort Robinson. The soldiers who had seen him fall had reported his death with certainty. Washington had accepted it.

But the Plains had never fully believed it.

Crazy Horse swung down from the saddle.

Red Cloud studied him for a moment.

"You took your time."

Crazy Horse allowed the faintest trace of a smile.

"I had to heal."

A few men laughed quietly. The tension broke like ice releasing on the river.

Quanah Parker stepped closer.

"The east believes you are dead."

Crazy Horse shrugged slightly.

"That helped."

Mato watched everything—the posture of the leaders, the quiet understanding between them, the way the gathering crowd seemed to breathe again.

He reached automatically for the folded paper in his coat.

Then hesitated.

Paper captured words. But this moment felt older than words.

He looked back toward the telegraph office. The wire hummed in the wind. Sound could carry news faster than riders now.

If the United States needed proof that the Plains still had leaders, proof could travel east before sunset.

Crazy Horse followed Mato's gaze.

"You are learning the wire."

Mato nodded. "It carries words farther than horses."

Crazy Horse considered that for a moment.

"Then send them."

Inside the telegraph room the operator looked uneasy when Mato entered.

"What message?"

Mato thought for a moment. Then he placed his fingers on the key.

Click.

Pause.

Click-click.

The operator listened carefully as Mato spoke the words aloud so he could send them correctly.

CRAZY HORSE PRESENT AT FORT LARAMIE.

ALIVE.

NO HOSTILE ACTION.

The key clicked steadily. The message moved east along the wire.

Outside the fort the wind moved across the open parade ground as it always had.

But something had changed.

Rumor had ended.

Now there was proof.

* * *

The message reached Washington before midnight.

Telegraph operators along the Platte passed it east without delay. The wire carried the words across Nebraska, across Iowa, and through the crowded industrial corridors of Illinois and Ohio until they arrived at the War Department office where clerks still worked beneath dim lamps.

The message was short.

CRAZY HORSE PRESENT AT FORT LARAMIE.

ALIVE.

NO HOSTILE ACTION.

The clerk read it twice before carrying it upstairs.

Within minutes the folded strip of telegraph paper rested on the desk of Ulysses S. Grant.

Grant read it once.

Then again.

Around him the room remained quiet.

One of the officers finally spoke. "If this is accurate…"

Grant finished the thought.

"…then the Army buried the wrong certainty."

The officer nodded slowly.

"Or the Plains are staging theater."

Grant studied the map again.

The Plains leaders had already demonstrated something Washington had underestimated.

They understood narrative.

The Secretary of War leaned forward. "We will need confirmation."

Grant looked toward the man who had carried the Plains terms east.

Valentine McGillycuddy still stood near the end of the table.

"You will return west," Grant said.

McGillycuddy did not hesitate. "Yes, sir."

"You will confirm whether the man at Fort Laramie is in fact Crazy Horse." Grant paused. "And you will continue the negotiations."

Within twenty-four hours the doctor was back on a train heading toward the plains.

* * *

Three weeks later the wind across Fort Laramie carried the distant whistle of the approaching rail line.

Word of McGillycuddy' s return reached the fort before he did.

Mato watched the wagon roll across the open parade ground late in the afternoon. The doctor climbed down slowly, travel dust still clinging to his coat.

"You came back," Mato said.

McGillycuddy studied the young man carefully.

"I told them I would."

Mato nodded toward the barracks.

"They want you to see him."

The doctor did not ask who. He followed.

Inside the officer quarters that now served as meeting space, the leaders of the Plains had gathered again.

Red Cloud.

Spotted Tail.

Quanah Parker.

And standing near the window—

Crazy Horse.

Alive.

The doctor approached slowly. For a moment neither man spoke.

Then McGillycuddy reached out and pressed his fingers gently against the scar beneath Crazy Horse's ribs.

The wound had healed tightly.

But it was unmistakable.

The doctor exhaled softly.

"I was wrong," he said.

Crazy Horse shook his head.

"No. You told them what you believed."

Outside the room another discussion had begun. A trader from Cheyenne had arrived that morning carrying a wooden photography box strapped to the back of his wagon. Word had spread quickly.

Some believed a photograph would end the rumors instantly.

Others resisted the idea entirely.

Images carried power. Among the Lakota many believed a photograph captured more than appearance—it captured spirit.

Quanah spoke first.

"If the United States wants proof, we can give it."

Spotted Tail frowned. "Proof for them is not always good for us."

Red Cloud turned toward Crazy Horse.

"They say soldiers once took your picture at Fort Robinson."

Crazy Horse did not answer immediately.

Finally, he said quietly, "They tried."

The silence that followed held more meaning than explanation.

McGillycuddy understood immediately. Even if a photograph existed, it had never been accepted by the Plains.

"You do not need a photograph," the doctor said.

"Washington does."

"No," he replied calmly. "They need certainty."

He gestured toward Crazy Horse.

"And certainty is standing in front of them."

Mato watched the exchange carefully.

Paper could carry words.

Wire could carry sound.

But proof, he realized, still depended on presence.

He returned quietly to the telegraph room that evening.

The operator looked up.

"Another message?"

Mato nodded and placed his fingers on the key again.

This time his movements were steadier.

Click.

Pause.

Click-click.

The signal began its long journey east.

CONFIRMED BY DR. MCGILLYCUDDY.

CRAZY HORSE ALIVE.

NEGOTIATIONS CONTINUE.

Outside the fort the wind moved across the open plains.

Inside the telegraph office Mato wrote the same message onto paper.

And for the first time he understood something that would guide the rest of his life.

History did not survive because it was spoken.

It survived because someone wrote it down.

Chapter 22 - The Table

Night settled quietly over Fort Laramie.

Mato Ska sat outside the telegraph room with paper across his knees. Inside, the operator had shown him again how water pipes carried waste through the officers' building—no snow, no walk into the dark prairie. The convenience unsettled him. Some of the white men's tools felt unnatural. Others felt… useful.

Footsteps approached.

Crazy Horse sat beside him.

They watched the stars for a long moment before Mato spoke.

"How did you get the scar on your cheek?"

Crazy Horse touched the mark along his left cheek.

"A jealous man."

Mato waited.

"A woman named Black Buffalo Woman," Crazy Horse said quietly. "She had been promised to another man. No Water."

Mato nodded.

"He believed I had taken what belonged to him."

"Had you?"

Crazy Horse looked toward the dark prairie.

"Love does not belong to anyone."

The words lingered between them.

"He shot at me," Crazy Horse said. "The bullet passed here."

He traced the scar along his cheek.

"He believed he killed me."

Mato smiled faintly. "Like the soldiers."

Crazy Horse nodded.

"Yes."

They sat in silence for a time. The telegraph wire hummed faintly in the wind.

"You are learning their tools," Crazy Horse said.

"Yes."

"Do you trust them?"

"They make some things easier."

Crazy Horse nodded slowly.

"Easier is not always better."

"I know."

"But some things are worth learning."

Crazy Horse studied him for a moment.

"You will remember things."

"I am trying."

Crazy Horse rose.

"Then remember this," he said quietly. "Love makes men foolish."

He walked away.

Mato remained outside the telegraph room long after, writing carefully by lantern light. Tomorrow the leaders would gather to decide the future of the Plains. Tonight, he simply recorded what the man had said.

* * *

Morning came clear over Fort Laramie.

Inside the former command building a long wooden table held a map of the continent. Around it stood Red Cloud, Spotted Tail, Quanah Parker, and leaders from the northern and southern plains.

Dr. Valentine McGillycuddy studied the map carefully.

Dakotas. Wyoming. Nebraska's western plains. Kansas grasslands. Indian Territory. The Texas Panhandle.

Not rebellion.

Geography.

At the edge of the room Mato wrote on both hide and paper. McGillycuddy noticed.

"You are writing both histories."

"I am trying."

Red Cloud spoke first.

"The river towns remain theirs."

He pointed along the Missouri.

"We do not want them."

Quanah Parker nodded.

"We want the land."

"The buffalo," Spotted Tail added.

"And no forts."

McGillycuddy listened carefully before responding.

"The rail corridors must remain open."

Quanah answered without hesitation.

"They may pass."

"But only by agreement."

Crazy Horse spoke quietly from the window.

"Then later they will ask again."

Permission.

Not surrender.

Mato wrote the word carefully.

Outside, the telegraph wire hummed in the wind. Inside the room men redrew the center of the continent.

For the first time Mato understood something that made his hand pause above the page.

He was not only recording history.

He was helping create it.

Chapter 23 - Washington Debates

Spring came unevenly to Washington, D.C.

Snow still clung to shaded streets while thaw turned the banks of the Potomac to mud. Inside the War Department, the long oak table was buried beneath maps.

Red circles marked forts no longer flying federal colors. Black lines tracked disrupted rail corridors. Blue pins clung stubbornly to remaining garrisons like islands in a receding tide.

Ulysses S. Grant stood at the head of the table without speaking.

The room was crowded: War Department officials, Interior Department representatives, railroad executives, a Reconstruction liaison from the South, and Dr. Valentine McGillycuddy, recently returned from the Plains.

The doctor's confirmation lay on the table before them.

Crazy Horse alive.

Negotiations continuing at Fort Laramie.

One of the railroad representatives broke the silence.

"You cannot allow this to stand."

Grant looked at him calmly. "Allow what?"

"A nation in the center of the continent."

Grant tapped the map.

"It already exists."

The man stiffened. Around the table several officials shifted uneasily.

The Secretary of War spoke carefully.

"If we reject their terms outright, we return to war."

Grant nodded slightly.

"And if we accept them?"

"We redefine the frontier."

The Reconstruction liaison finally spoke.

"If troops are pulled west in large numbers, the South destabilizes."

No one needed further explanation. Reconstruction remained fragile. Federal troops still stood between uneasy peace and renewed conflict.

Grant understood arithmetic better than most politicians.

The Army could fight the Plains.

But doing so might fracture the Union again.

He studied the map once more.

Dakotas.

Wyoming.

Nebraska.

Kansas.

Indian Territory.

The Texas Panhandle.

A continental spine.

For years Washington had believed it controlled that center of the continent. Now the pins on the map suggested otherwise.

The Plains were not raiding.

They were governing.

One of the railroad men leaned forward.

"If the Union Pacific cannot guarantee passage, investors will abandon western expansion."

Another voice added quietly, "And if the rail collapses, commerce collapses with it."

Grant folded his arms.

"They are not asking for our cities," he said. "They are asking for the land between them."

The room absorbed that.

A banker present at the meeting spoke cautiously.

"If rail remains open, commerce survives."

Grant nodded.

"And the Union survives."

He looked again toward the folded pages on the table—the terms carried east by McGillycuddy.

Recognition of Plains governance west of the Missouri.

Protection of buffalo herds.

Removal of federal forts.

Controlled rail corridors.

The center of the continent.

Not conquered.

Negotiated.

Grant rested his hand on the map.

"What do they want?" he asked.

"They have sent terms," someone replied quietly.

Grant considered them for a long moment.

He had commanded armies across a continent during the Civil War. He knew what it meant to destroy an enemy who refused compromise.

But he also knew the cost of doing so.

Finally, he spoke.

"Prepare the agreement."

The room fell silent.

Because everyone present understood what that meant.

For the first time since Appomattox, the United States would not be dictating terms.

It would be answering them.

Epilogue (Book One) - A Young Man Reads the Map

New York - Autumn, 1887

The map did not look like the others.

It hung on the wall of a small study cluttered with books, hunting trophies, and unfinished manuscripts. Most maps of the United States showed a familiar shape—states spreading steadily westward across the continent.

This one was different.

Across the center of the country, stretching from the Dakotas to the Texas Panhandle, another color appeared. The cartographer had labeled it carefully:

Plains Confederation.

A young man stood before the map with his hands resting on his hips.

Theodore Roosevelt studied it with fascination.

"Remarkable," he murmured.

He leaned closer.

Rail corridors were marked with thin black lines. Federal territory remained to the east. But the center of the continent—the old frontier—now belonged to something entirely new.

An Indian nation.

He tapped the map lightly with his finger.

"They held it."

Roosevelt was not surprised that the tribes had fought. History was full of such struggles.

What interested him was something else entirely.

They had won.

And then they had governed.

Few nations managed the second part.

A letter lay open on the desk behind him. It came from a railroad associate who had recently traveled west through Nebraska. The letter described the frontier as it now existed: buffalo herds returning under tribal protection, rail lines crossing the Plains under negotiated corridors, American forts abandoned or dismantled, and telegraph wires still humming across territory Washington did not control.

Roosevelt smiled slightly.

"Extraordinary."

He picked up a pencil and made a small mark along the Missouri River.

"No nation remains still forever," he said quietly.

Roosevelt had no desire to destroy the Plains nation. But he understood something many Americans did not yet grasp.

A sovereign power now existed in the middle of North America.

And sooner or later the United States would have to decide what to do about it.

He rolled the map carefully and set it aside.

Outside the window, New York traffic rattled through the street. Across the continent, the wind moved steadily over the plains. Somewhere beyond the Missouri River a new flag flew above the old fort at Fort Laramie.

Roosevelt smiled again.

"I believe," he said quietly,

"I should see this place for myself."

A new nation had risen—and the world had not yet reckoned with it.

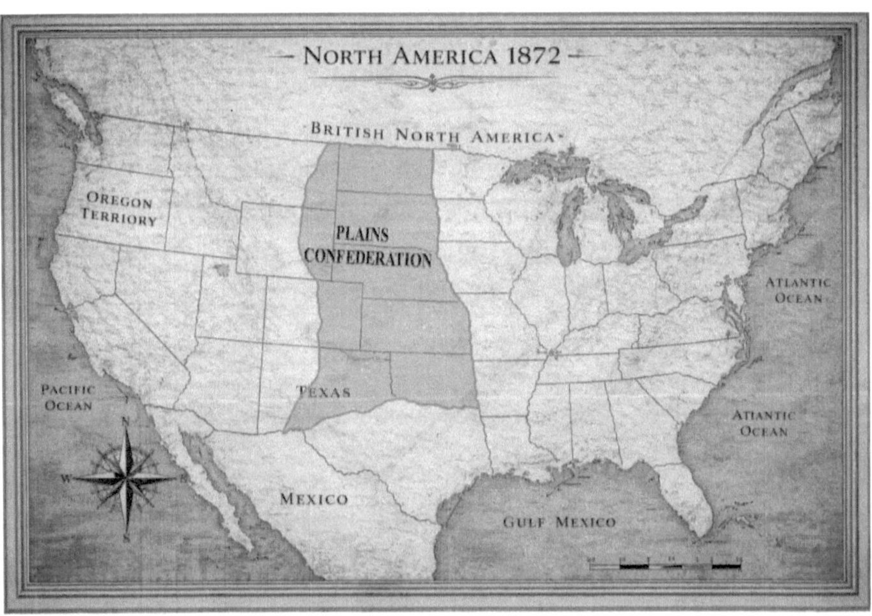

Continue the Story…

The Plains Confederation has been born—but survival is far from certain.

As leaders struggle to hold together a fragile alliance of nations, new threats begin to rise from within and beyond their borders. The United States watches closely. Other powers begin to take interest. And the cost of sovereignty may demand more than unity alone.

The story of the Plains has only just begun.

Book Two of the Nations of the Plains series is coming soon.

Also, by Alan Maas

If you enjoyed A Nation Without Reservation, you may also like:

The Kind Legacy Series
A historical Western saga of family, mystery, and survival in the Dakota Territory and the Black Hills—where history and legend intertwine across generations.

Available on Amazon.

www.ingramcontent.com/pod-product-compliance
Lightning Source LLC
LaVergne TN
LVHW090525110826
845146LV00003B/984

* 9 7 9 8 9 8 9 0 6 6 0 6 3 *